TWOFOLD

BY

SEXY

Sexy

Twofold by Sexy

Copyright© 2007 by Deborah Cardona
Déjà Vu Publications

The library of congress has cataloged the soft cover edition as follows:

Cardona, Deborah
Twofold
ISBN Number: 978-1-60402-598-9 (13-digit)

Cover Design by: Marion Designs
Editing and Typesetting by: Carla M. Dean,
                             U Can Mark My Word

Sales inquiries should be forwarded to:
Déjà Vu Publications
P.O. Box 1002
New York, N.Y. 10029

Dedicated to

My four sons

Marcus, David, Angel, and Damion

Sexy

Acknowledgements

It is times like this when I sit down to think about all the people I should and want to thank. The list is long; believe me when I say I have had a lot of support from family and friends. So where do I begin.

First, I would like to thank GOD for giving me the gift to express myself through words. He has blessed me with a new life and I'm going to do my best to show my appreciation.

I would like to thank everyone who believed in me when I didn't believe in myself. I would also like to thank those that didn't; you guys are the ones who pushed me to prove my point. The points being never allow anyone to kill your dream of becoming successful. My people (you know who you are) the 100th Street Crew thanks for all of your support.

My other half, I know I put you through a lot of changes; it's all part of the separation. We will either survive it or go our separate ways. I doubt the latter because our love is too strong.

The Cardona Family, I love you. Mom, Tyo, and Papa, I know you are looking down at me and showering me with your blessings (RIP).To my brothers, Ray, Tuto, and Angel, you guys have been there since day one and believed I could be that bitch...ride or die bitch, that is. Thank you for always looking out for me and the kids.

My personal assistance, Carmen, thanks for letting me hire you. You taught me a great deal. Patti, my comia, I adore you. You have always been there for me through the good and bad times. Rosie, you know I have mad love for you; life gets better with time. China, you know you are my homey. All those tears do not go unnoticed; I love you.

5

Sexy

Trouble & P.R., the party has just begun. We've seen some hard times, and through it all, you both have remained true. Thank you for always being there. I love u both dearly. Bebe, once again I say hurry home. TiTi misses you.

My Mom and Dad Padilla, thank you for all you have done for me. Mom and Dad Castro, thank you for everything. The Negron Family, thanks. The Mateo Family, thanks for all the support.

To Kwan, author of *Still Hood,* thank you for all the love and support. To Treasure E. Blue, author of *Harlem Girl Lost,* thank you for always guiding me in the right direction. To Miz, author of *Bishop,* thank you for taking me under your wing. Make Money!!! To my dear friend Lester Ricks from the Harlem Book Center, thank you for pushing my books out there. At every turn, I find my books at the stands.

And to my readers, I hope that you will enjoy this book. Thank you so much for all the love.

Love is Love!

Sexy

TWOFOLD

BY

SEXY

Sexy

Chapter 1

How can two brothers be so different and yet so much alike?

Damion asked himself that question so many times throughout the years. His twin brother, Devon, was the complete opposite of him in so many ways, yet when they looked at each other, they saw the same face. Outside of their resemblance, their outlook on life was totally different. The only thing that kept them connected since they began to build on their own ideas and opinions was their ambition to make it out of the projects, where they had ended up when their mother Jaz decided to stop hustling on the streets of New York City.

She had raised her sons in the hood, worked two jobs, and sometimes did without the extra funds she was use to making out on the street. The money and luxuries at the time were good to both her and Trouble, the childhood friend she had learned to trust with everything she had, including her sons, but the consequences were not worth the risk. Jaz wanted her sons to grow up with values. She didn't want them to be spoiled little hustler boys like the ones she often came across in the hood, who sat around the projects wearing one-hundred-dollar sneakers and bragging about whose father or mother held the highest position in their crew of drug dealers. She wanted her sons to appreciate the value of a dollar and become educated in a special field, but most importantly, she wanted them to value family.

Washington Projects, where Jaz made their home, was one of the worst in Spanish Harlem. On the corner of 100th Street and 3rd Avenue, base heads and dope fiends alike lurked around every corner, inside stairwells, and on elevators. They had taken ownership. Day in and day out, they could be seen running around the neighborhood smoking out of their glass pipes, while scheming on how to get their next hit. Out in the open, they conducted transactions with no regard to the families who worked harder than most to keep the poison away from their seeds. It was extremely difficult for the neighborhood kids to live a normal lifestyle, especially in the "D", the park in the Washington Projects.

Damion can remember walking to and from school with great expectations of one day making it out of there. The empty crack vials that were disposed of so freely throughout the schoolyard were just an added bonus, which only inspired him to do better for himself. Unfortunately, his twin, Devon, wanted to be a part of the ghetto life, but that was then. Because of his brother's choices, Damion now had to make trips up to Sing-Sing Correctional Facility, where his other half was doing a 25-to-life bid.

Damion now lived in the suburbs on a quiet street where the children played without any concerns. He drove a $50,000 Lexus SUV and worked for a prestigious accounting firm in midtown Manhattan. He earned close to $100,000 a year, and life was good. The struggles he endured to get where he was today had not been easy. There were times while growing up that he thought he wouldn't make it out of the hell he lived in. That's when his brother would step up to the plate. Devon was always there to remind him of their goal. He would always tell Damion how important it was for him to get an education and then a career. For Damion getting a degree was a must, unlike Devon, who had dropped out of high school and changed his choice of professions.

Damion stood looking out of his office window, as memories of his past danced around in his head. He stared down at a dazzling view of New York City, a city of opportunity, a city where one could fulfill one's dreams... dreams one could make a reality when desire and determination overrode anything else in life.

As he unbuttoned the top button of his collared shirt, Damion began to think about the day when all of his brother's opportunities had come to an end, the day both of their lives had changed. He could remember that day as if it were yesterday.

"Yo, Damion, what the fuck are you doing home sleeping? Don't you have classes today?" Devon asked, as he stood in front of his bed like a drill sergeant.

"Yeah, man," Damion responded, wiping the sleep from his eyes.

"Well, get your ass up."

"Why is it that I'm the only one around here that has to go to school? Can you answer that for me? You think I don't know what you're doing."

"I don't know what you're talking about," Devon said, while trying to pull the covers from over Damion's head.

"Stop, man, I'm fuckin' tired. I was up till three o'clock this morning studying."

Damion was starting to feel the pressure of his studies. To maintain an 'A' average he had to go the extra mile in his classes. His eyes felt heavy as the sun tried to peek beneath his comforter. So, at this point, all he wanted was sleep.

One day won't stop no show, he thought, as his brother continued to harass him.

"Why is it that you're always asking stupid questions? Just get your ass up. I need to talk to you."

Hearing the urgency in his brother's voice, Damion knew it had to be something serious. So, he sat up, pushed the

11

covers off, and swung his legs off the bed. Finding that his third leg was at attention, he immediately ran to the bathroom to relieve himself and to brush his pearly whites. When finished, Damion walked back into the bedroom, where he noticed Devon on his knees looking for something underneath his bed. When Devon heard Damion moving around in the background, he looked up and found himself looking directly into his brother's face.

Still, after all the years of being mistaken for one another, Devon couldn't help but to smile at Damion. It was scary. With their year-round tans and their eyes the same color as their mother's, they were considered the finest niggas in the projects. And they knew it. They sported the same czars and goatees, stood 5'9" tall, and weighed in at about 180 pounds each. The only difference between them was a birthmark, which Damion had on his left thigh. Other than that they were identical.

Devon couldn't believe how time had passed him by. As he looked at his twin, he realized he had to be honest with him. He had to give him the heads-up on his new ventures. They had shared everything while growing up—all of their secrets, dreams, and visions. There had been no secrets between them until now.

Devon had stopped going to school about six months ago. Yeah, he would go to the school grounds; however, he never made it inside. Devon would wait until Damion was out of sight to begin his day as a drug pusher. He was fully aware that he was betraying his family and all the values his mother had instilled in him. But once he got past that first day, he was hooked.

Damion had started noticing changes in Devon right away. But when asked what was going on with him, Devon would brush the questions off by changing the subject. His intentions were never to deceive his brother. He just didn't want him to look down on him. Devon always knew that the right time would come eventually, when he would have to tell his brother the truth. Now, six months later, he found that it was time to reveal the ins and outs of his criminal activities. Devon stood directly in front of Damion with a metal box in his hand.

"Open it," Devon ordered, handing the box over with a key.

"Don't be barking at me. It's too fuckin' early in the morning for this bullshit, Dee."

"Yeah, whatever, man, just open the box. All of your questions will be answered."

Damion was curious to know what his brother was up to. He had heard rumors that Devon was out on the streets hustling—selling crack cocaine, but he didn't want to believe that. His theory was that his brother was just bored with school. At least that was what he wanted to believe. Dey, as he was nicknamed, knew his brother well enough to know that eventually he would tell him. He had waited for this moment. Finally, Devon was going to share his secret.

Damion grabbed the box and placed it on the wooden desk he used for studying. He inserted the key into the keyhole, turned it to the left, and there in front of his eyes, he saw a .357 Magnum, stacks of hundred dollar bills, and a set of keys. Damion was speechless. Now there was no doubt in his mind. His brother was out there slinging crack. There was only one question he wanted answered. He wanted to know who had turned his brother out to the game.

Devon was ready to answer all of Damion's questions, but instead Damion fell silent. The look on Damion's face was not what he had expected. His nose became as cold as ice; his body froze from the fear of what Damion might say.

Devon couldn't quite put into words how he had gotten involved in the drug game. However, he knew he had to explain his actions in full detail. His brother deserved to know the truth regardless of how he would feel. After a few seconds of contemplating, Devon asked his brother to say something.

Sexy

Damion couldn't put into words the disappointment he felt in his brother. The anger was beyond anything he had ever experienced. The fire that burned inside of him caused his body to shiver. He didn't have words for Devon, so instead, he turned around, dropped the box to the floor, and commenced to whipping Devon's ass.

After all these years, Damion still found that shit funny. What he didn't find funny was the fact that after the ass whipping, Devon continued in his life of crime, becoming one of the biggest hustlers in Spanish Harlem. He had 100th Street locked down.

At the age of twenty-one, Devon had it all—money, cars, women, and respect. What he didn't have was self-control, something a nigga needed to maintain. The codes of the street were about respect no matter what the cost. Money gave him all of that. The only thing money couldn't buy Devon was his freedom card.

Damion still remembered clearly the day his brother lost his life to the system, the day they all lost their lives to the system. It was the night that their Aunt Trouble married her hustling partner, Lover Lizard. Damion was asked by one of the waitresses at Club Ecstasy to inform the gentleman at the door that they were closed for the evening. The waitress had been unable to control the gentleman, who insisted on speaking to someone in management. He just wouldn't take "no" for an answer. Damion, who had plans to continue partying along with everyone else, walked over to the entrance in hopes of settling the situation quickly. However, it was too late.

He never got the chance to see who was at the door. All Damion remembered was the sound of gunshots that were spraying in his direction and heard throughout the club. Even with the music playing, his family was able to redirect their steps and head toward the sound. It's strange that anyone would want to run into the line of fire; however, he was grateful they did. If not, he would have been dead.

Jaz was the first one to arrive at her son's side. She gently touched him, frantically searching for signs of life. Then, she started to scream as she turned her head and saw the body of another young man lying out on the sidewalk in a pool of blood.

"What the fuck just happened?" was all she was able to say.

Devon had grabbed her by the arm and pushed her back into the club.

"Mom, chill! Everything is alright. Damion is alright. Stay here. Please go back inside and wait for me."

Jaz looked into Devon's eyes. His stern stare assured her that he had everything under control. She turned slowly into the club and into the arms of her lover Toni.

Devon bent down and whispered into Damion's ear, "You can get up now. Everything's okay."

As Jaz looked on, she noticed that Devon had a gun in his hand. She wanted so much to reach out to him, but couldn't. She was stuck. Jaz couldn't believe her eyes. All she thought about was their late-night talks about the streets. She had never hidden her past from them. No matter what, she always kept it real. They had deserved that much from her. Now, her past was staring her in the face.

She watched as Damion lifted himself from the floor, brushed his suit off, and then embraced Devon as though his life depended on it. After they checked each other out, they turned in union to look at their mother. Jaz felt like an ass whipping was coming on for them scaring the shit out of her. But instead, she opened her arms and thanked God for keeping her babies safe, which was all that mattered at that moment.

It never dawned on her that their lives would be changed forever. One of her sons would be charged with murder in the first degree.

Sexy

Chapter 2

Time was at a standstill for Devon. Four years into his bid and he still felt unsettled. Always having to be on his Ps and Qs about everything aggravated him. Being at Sing-Sing Correctional was a lot like being on the street. He never had time to just kick back and relax. In the max joint, where he found himself confined, he had to fight to survive. Mostly he fought to keep his sanity. Since the day he killed one of the Supreme's boys, he tried to maintain a sense of peace.

Damion was not aware that Supreme had put a price tag on Devon's head. Devon didn't know anything about it either for that matter. It was a surprise to them both. The fucked up part was that the hit man had no idea that he was trying to kill the wrong man. Anyone who didn't know there was a twin could have mistaken them at any point.

Devon's first instinct was to protect his older brother. He was the one that lived his life according to the rules. Damion had accomplished so much in life, and Devon couldn't allow his lifestyle to interfere with what Damion was trying to do with his. Besides, their mother had made it clear to them both that they should always take care and protect each other.

Because of their connection as twins, their bond, but most of all their loyalty, was much stronger than that of any other sibling. All they had was each other. Yeah, they had their mother, who was an O.G., and her lover Toni to guide them through life, but they could never begin to understand or share in the bond the twin brothers managed to maintain.

Still after all this time, Devon wasn't able to adjust to prison life. He felt there was some unfinished business he needed to attend to. Supreme had been the one that maintained the product and the spot where they distributed dime bags of crack cocaine. He taught Devon everything he needed to know about the business...how to cook, cut, and bag the coca. However, somewhere along the way, Devon decided to go out on his own. Devon understood where all the animosity came from. Supreme felt betrayed.

The morning Devon shared his secret, Damion made it a point of letting Devon know he didn't agree with him. He also made it known that if Devon was going to be out there hustling, he was never to make the next nigga rich. Devon could recall his brother's words clearly.

"Never, and I mean never, make the next nigga rich, fool. If this is what you really want to do, then you better represent."

Devon had to smile at the thought. Those words were told to him right after Damion put the beats on him. No matter what the situation, right, wrong, or indifferent, Damion always had his back, not only as his brother but as his friend, too. On that, Devon could depend.

When Supreme found out that Devon had started hustling on 100th Street between Third Avenue and Lexington, he confronted him straight up.

"Yo, what's good, man? I heard you were out here doing your own thing," Supreme questioned Devon, as the veins in his neck pumped fire.

"Yeah. Why?"

"Why, nigga? You know you playin' yourself. What the fuck do you think you're doing?"

Devon and Supreme were standing face to face, so close that they could feel each other's breath, their hungry eyes never losing sight of each other. It didn't matter who else was around. This was personal. Devon had already been informed that this confrontation was about to take place, so he was ready.

"Since when did you become an entrepreneur?"

"Since the day I realized I could be a very rich man," Devon stated, as he moved in closer.

"Oh, you got jokes."

"Nah, I ain't got no jokes. I'm just keeping it real."

"Dee, don't step on my motherfuckin' toes, man. You my boy and all, but business is business. Plus, I don't think you ready to fuck with the big boys."

"Listen, Sup. I ain't tryin' to step on nobody's toes. I got to do what I got to do. We can both get paid."

"You think?"

"Yeah."

"Yeah, alright, but if you start playin' outside your league and my money flow gets low, then we're going to have problems."

"Yo, you threatening me? I thought we were boys," Devon asked Supreme, with a little confusion in his tone.

"Don't be so naïve. This shit ain't personal. This is business."

Deciding to be easy, Supreme backed up. At the moment, he needed to know at all times where Devon's state of mind was at.

"Whatever, dawg," Devon replied, while backing up, also.

However, this little setback was not going to stop him from hustling. If Supreme felt threatened, then he would have to deal with his own issues. Devon had plans to become extremely confident in his quest. He wanted to do what his mother had given up. He wanted to become a strong hustler like his Aunt Trouble, and wealthy beyond his wildest dreams.

Things didn't turn out quite as he had planned, though. Time had left a gap for so many questions that were still unanswered. Devon sat in his cell wondering how he was going to get through the next twenty-one years taming the beast that lived inside of him.

He got up from his bunk to look into the mirror that hung several inches above the sink and toilet. What he saw looking back was a young brother who had made all the wrong choices. Because of where he was he had to maintain a certain balance. Strength and independence were two of the main things niggas looked upon in the P-Nile. This wasn't a place for weakness, regardless of how hurt he might feel over his situation. There were days when he just wanted to crawl into his mother's bed and feel her arms wrapped around him, as he had so many times while growing up.

* * * * *

Damion continued to look out his office window. Suddenly, he became sad. He was waiting for Devon's attorney to return his phone call. Devon's first appeal was going in front of a judge today. Hopefully, he would grant in favor of Devon. There were no self-defense laws in New York State, so murder was murder any way you sliced it. The appeal was not guaranteed, but that didn't stop the attorney from finding grounds to appeal Devon's sentence.

Damion had testified at his brother's first trial. He described step by step how Devon had killed to protect him. Devon had put his life on the line for him. He explained to the jury that he owed his life to his brother, and Damion wasn't lying when he said those words. He was not ready to hang up the gloves yet. That is why he was going to make sure Devon had the best defense lawyers New York had to offer.

Being snapped back into his current reality by his secretary's voice, Damion had to deal with the here and now.

"Mr. Aviles, you have a call on Line 1. It's Mr. Padilla."

"Thank you, Jane. I'll take it. Can you please hold all my other calls?"

"Yes, sir."

"Mr. Padilla, thank you for returning my call so quickly. How's it going?"

"Well, Damion, I need to be completely honest with you."

Isn't that why I pay you so much fuckin' money, to tell me the truth, Damion thought to himself.

"Things aren't looking so good. The judge took a glance at the appeal and set a date. But that's not the problem. The problem is that he just glanced at it. He didn't look a bit interested in the case."

"What is that supposed to mean?"

"It means that the appeal will be heard, but it is unlikely it will be granted."

Damion was not trying to hear that shit. He had paid Mr. Padilla enough money in hopes of getting the conviction overturned. Now he was giving him this bullshit line.

"Mr. Padilla, listen. I don't know what's going on. The truth of the matter is I'm really not trying to hear anything negative. I need someone who is going to fight for my brother's life."

"Damion, I understand. Please know that I am going to do my best, the very best I can do."

"Well, your best isn't good enough."

Damion's tone was level. All he wanted was to make his point clear.

"Mr. Aviles, you have a call on Line 2," Jane announced through the intercom.

"Didn't I tell you to hold all of my fuckin' calls?"

Damion was losing it. The latest update on his brother's case was taking its toll.

"It's your mother, Damion, and don't you ever talk to me like that again."

Jane was fully aware of what Damion was going through. However, she wasn't going to allow him to disrespect her.

"Okay, okay, please ask her to hold on," he replied, quickly changing his tone.

Damion had to regroup. He was on an emotional roller coaster.

"Mr. Padilla, just let me know the date and time of the hearing. I have to take another call."

Damion scribbled the information onto his calendar, and then switched over without so much as thanking the attorney. He needed to talk to the most important woman in his life. She would know exactly what needed to be said in order for him to feel better. Damion was blessed that he was raised by such a strong woman. Not only was she strong, but she was also an intelligent, loving, caring, and devoted mother. Jaz was everything.

"Hi, Mom. What's up?"

"Hi, baby. I just wanted to talk to you. Hear your voice. How are things going? I hadn't heard from you today. Thought maybe something was wrong."

Damion and Devon had made it a habit of calling Jaz every morning. They didn't need a reason. It was what it was.

"Damn, Mom, I'm sorry. It slipped my mind. I've been so busy thinking about Devon and the appeal that time passed me by."

"It's okay, Dey. So how's it going? Have you heard anything yet?"

Jaz always spoke with a soft tone. She held magic in her voice. The peaceful serene song she sung always made him relax, and he needed that special touch right about now.

"I just got off the phone with one of his attorneys. He mentioned something about how the judge from the Court of Appeals barely looked at the briefs or motions. Nothing will be known until the day of the hearing," Damion replied, while letting out a sigh of defeat.

"Damion, I know you have put your all into your brother's release. But, you really need to start taking care of yourself. You are neither guilty nor responsible for your brother's incarceration. The only thing we can do is pray, unless for some strange reason, Supreme admits that he hired someone to kill your brother."

"Mom, I know you're right, but you know better than anyone how I feel about my brother. He is a part of me. So, until he is free, I will not rest."

"Okay, I understand. So what's next? As a matter of fact, don't answer that. Why don't you call your Aunt Trouble, and ask her to give you the name and number of the lawyers who helped get Lissy out?"

"What did he do? Get her a time cut, right?"

"Yeah, but it's better than nothing. Anyway, you decide."

"Okay, Mom. I love you."

"Me, too, baby."

Damion replaced the phone in its cradle, and then pushed the intercom button. "Jane, can you please get my Aunt Trouble on the line for me?"

"No problem, Dey."

Damion sat back in his chair and waited for the call to go through.

Sexy

Chapter 3

Jaz and Trouble had decided once the boys came along to let the Geechies hold down the spot. That way Trouble could go back to school, receive her degree in fashion, and open up her own boutique. While Jaz focused on raising the twins, their street business was still booming. The money was good, but the risks of getting incarcerated were high. So, they decided to let it go once Club Ecstasy opened for business.

"Good afternoon, Desires. Lissy speaking."

"What's up, pretty lady? Is my aunt there?"

"Hi, Dey. How are you, kid?"

"Lissy, please, I am not a kid anymore."

"Well, baby, I'm sorry to inform you that you will always be a cute little kid to me."

"Whatever. Is she there?"

"Yes, she is, but before I get her, how's Devon doing?"

"He's great, Lissy, just fuckin' great. He's sitting behind bars," Damion barked into the receiver.

"Hold up, Dey. You don't need to be disrespectful toward me. I am not the enemy here. You should have a little more respect for me, you know. I've known you since you were born. As a matter of fact, I used to change your dirty diapers."

Hurt over Damion's verbal attack, Lissy had to catch her breath.

"My bad, Lissy. Please forgive me. I don't know what's gotten into me lately. I'm so fuckin' stressed out behind all this shit."

"I understand that you're angry, Dey, but you need to remember we are all on the same side. Hold your head. Wait a minute. Let me go get Trouble for you."

Lissy understood more than Damion imagined. She had been separated from the only family she had ever known, too.

"Thanks, Lissy."

Damion found that whenever confronted by his brother's situation, he became bitter. He had to find a better way to deal. Damion took a deep breath, counted to ten, and waited for Trouble to pick up the line.

"Hello, Dey. Are you there? I can hear you breathing. What's wrong, baby?" Trouble asked in an alarmed tone.

These boys meant the world to her. They were very much a part of her, too. She could always tell when there was something wrong with them by their behavior or the sound of their voices. Now was one of those times. She would live with the memory of her wedding day forever. It was the happiest day as well as the saddest day of her life.

"Hey, Titi, listen. I'm calling because my mom asked me to. I need the name and number of the attorney you used in Lissy's case."

"Sure, baby, not a problem. You got a pen?"

After Trouble gave Damion the information, she thought it would be the perfect opportunity to invite him over for dinner. Maybe a night out among family and friends would make him feel better. He needed to know that he was not alone in all of this.

"I would love to come over, but tonight isn't a good night. I'll take a rain check, though."

"Alright, Damion. I want you to know that I'm here for you if you need me."

"Thanks, Titi, but I think I got everything I need for the moment."

Damion was already feeling better. Everything he needed he held in his hand. Hopefully, the attorney he was about to call would be a little more enthusiastic about Devon's appeal.

* * * * *

Meanwhile back at Sing-Sing, Devon grew anxious. He knew there would be a waiting period, but all the waiting was stressing him out. Damion would get word to him soon. On that, he could always depend, he thought to himself, while slowly turning away from the bars that separated him from the other inmates.

He walked over to his bunk, lowered himself to his knees, and prayed. Once he felt that he had become connected to his higher power, he got up, pulled his wife beater over his shoulders, and caressed his six-pack. Since his incarceration, Devon had spent most of his time at the gym or in the yard working out. He learned early on in his bid that in order to maintain his sanity, he had to stay busy. Attending educational and work programs were the most productive; working out and meditations were the best motivators. Outside of that, most men looked forward to the V.I.'s they received from the females in their lives. If they didn't have a significant other, then they waited on their mothers. That's what they considered therapy for the mind.

Devon thought about how his mother was one of those women who came up on every visit, lugging food packages and a smile. It hurt him deeply to have his mother go through that experience. After those visits, his mother's pained face never left his mind—only to remind him of the disappointment for the next V.I.

Devon lowered himself onto the cold tiles of his cell, and began doing push-ups non-stop. Sweat ran down his face along with a few tears. When his body screamed "Enough," he got up to look into the mirror again. What he saw now was a man of strength, a man that could overcome all the obstacles that stood in his way. After grabbing his shower slippers and robe, he headed for the showers.

Devon walked down the corridor, a passageway that led to different areas of the block. At the shower entrance, he noticed a group of guys standing around laughing. The biggest man in the group called out to Devon—waving his hands, desperately trying to get his attention.

"Hey, my nigga. What's good? I heard you're waiting on news about your appeal," Marcus said, approaching Devon.

"Yeah, Big Man. I should be hearing something real soon."

Big Man, whose real name was Marcus Redding, had gotten acquainted with Devon while riding up to Sing-Sing. Because of Marcus's huge physique and scarred face, no one wanted to sit next to him, so Devon got stuck being that there were no other seats available. When he climbed onto the iron horse, he had no choice. By the look on Marcus's face, Devon figured he didn't want to be bothered, and that was okay with him. Devon wasn't up to conversing with anyone anyway. Marcus stared out of the window acknowledging no one.

Devon was overwhelmed with fear—not of the man who sat beside him, but of the unknown. The stories he had heard of prison life throughout his youth made him remorseful of the choices he had made. However, Devon refused to cry over spilled milk now. He had no choice but to take this time in stride, pray for the best, and work night and day on his appeal.

They rode on the Upstate Thruway for thirty minutes in silence, each man in his own thoughts. The sound of the tires on the road's pavement was getting to him. With the voices in his head becoming louder and unbearable, Devon wanted to strike up a conversation with the man beside him. After a few minutes of contemplating, he decided to go for it. The worst that could happen was he would have his first showdown on his way to the pen.

"Hey, man, what's up? Is this your first ride up North?"

Devon held his breath. For a little extra assurance, he crossed his fingers, too. Devon was a laidback individual. He wasn't in no mood for any unnecessary bullshit. If the nigga played himself, he would have to unleash the beast. Like everyone else in the game, Devon had an explosive side to him. By the time they reached Sing-Sing Correctional Facility, Devon was surprised that Marcus was not at all what he seemed. Looks were deceiving. He wasn't a notorious serial killer. He was the complete opposite. He was more like a big teddy bear.

Devon was able to get a lot out of Marcus. Like Devon, this was also his first time up North. Yeah, he had done a few city bids at Riker's Island, but nothing serious. Since that first day, they had become the best of friends. Fortunately for Devon, his first few years went smoothly with Marcus at his side. No one ever dared to cross the line. Their rep followed them wherever they went. Marcus had intimidated some of the toughest convicts in the system, making Devon's time a lot easier. He never had to worry about the violence that hid behind the shadows of the prison walls.

"Yo, I hope everything works out for you."

Devon nodded in agreement. He had to get out of there. For days, he thought about ways that he could escape. Devon wanted to throw the idea at Marcus, but he wasn't sure Marcus could be trusted with that type of information. A nigga had to have limitations on his friendships. Besides, he didn't want Marcus to think he was weak and couldn't do time.

He looked at Marcus in deep thought. He was going to need him if he decided to go through with it. Devon stretched out his arm and patted Marcus on the shoulder.

"Thanks, man. To be honest, I'm not getting my hopes up. You know it can take years for an appeal to come through. Some of these old timers have been at it a long time," Devon stated, as he put his arm around Marcus, guiding him to the shower area.

Marcus looked at Devon strangely. "What's up, kid? You look like you got something else on your mind."

"Listen, Big Man. I've been debating with myself about telling you something."

"What, man? You know you can tell me anything."

"First, you got to give me your word as a man that this will go no further. Also, you can't question me."

"What's good, dawg? Someone fuckin' with you? What, you want me to take somebody out?"

"Nah, it's deeper than that. And besides, what you gonna do with your soft ass?" Devon pushed Marcus playfully.

"Why you trying to play me, Dee? You know you my dawg. I'll go out for you," Marcus replied, while holding his fist over his heart.

"Yeah, I know, but it's not about getting at anybody in here. Just meet me tonight at the yard. There are a few things I want to run your way, and now is not a good time. Besides, we got some ear hustlers lurking around."

"Alright, man. I'll be there. What time?"

"Eight o'clock."

Devon walked off, hoping he was doing the right thing. Niggas tended to flip when the pressure was on.

Chapter 4

Damion was preparing for a meeting that had been called by the senior partners at the last minute. Didn't they realize he had phone calls to make? He was not in the mood to be around a bunch of stuffed shirts when he had more important things to do. Maybe he would ask for a few days off.

Damion really needed time to deal with his personal problems without having to worry about work. He grabbed his briefcase, walked over to his file cabinet, and removed the file his boss had requested. Before he opened the door to leave, he looked back. He noticed all of the blinking lights on his phone. Those calls were his lifeline—his bread and butter. For how long, he wasn't sure. Things were really getting hectic.

He had not heard back from the attorney. Maybe he had been a bit harsh. As a second thought, he walked out of the office and straight towards the conference room. When he walked in, he noticed how everyone directly involved with this particular account was waiting on his arrival.

"So nice of you to join us, Mr. Aviles," Senior Partner Sterling greeted him, with annoyance in his voice.

"Sorry I'm late, sir. I was waiting for an important phone call concerning the Wilshire account," Damion said, as he took his seat at the table and looked directly at his boss.

"Well, we can now get started. Damion, did you bring the new profile I requested?"

"Yes, sir."

Damion handed the file over to Mr. Sterling, and then his mind traveled. He couldn't get his brother out of his head. Damion and Devon had a way of communicating. It was a rare mental telepathy kind of thing. He couldn't explain it. Damion drifted off, when he was suddenly awakened by Mr. Sterling's voice.

"Damion. Damiooon!"

"Oh shit, yes, sir."

"Are you alright? I've been sensing some problems from you lately."

"No, sir, I'm not alright. Would you mind if I spoke to you in private, sir? It's important. May we go out to the hall?"

Damion felt embarrassed that it had come to this, as he waited for Sterling to give him the okay. When he realized his boss was in agreement with his request, he relaxed, pushed his chair away from the table, excused himself, and then rose. Once out of earshot of the others, he explained he needed to take some time off to handle some personal issues. He wasn't sure if it was wise to tell Mr. Sterling the truth about his brother, but what choice did he have if asked? Being that he was one of the few who had made it out of the projects, he refused to jeopardize his job by being honest. His brother's criminal activities were not something he could bring to his place of employment.

"Well, Damion, I must say that you have done an excellent job with this portfolio," Mr. Sterling stated, while shuffling through the file. "I don't have a problem with you taking a leave of absence. However, I am extremely concerned with the matter at hand."

Damion sighed as he lifted his head to look at the gentleman before him—the man who had given him his first break at a real life.

"I know you haven't been yourself lately. I also know that your brother is part of the problem. Why don't we go into my office so we can talk?"

"But, sir, your meeting."

"Oh yeah, that can wait. We have much more important issues to address," Sterling replied, going beyond the call of duty.

Damion couldn't believe how everything was playing out. He broke the story down to Mr. Sterling, who sat at his desk with his mouth open. He was amazed at how Damion had made all of the right choices no matter what his obstacles had been. He was impressed with the young man who sat before him. He was especially proud to have a young man such as this working at his company. He knew then that he had made the right choice in hiring Damion.

They spoke for a good portion of the morning without any interruptions. When Damion finally came to the end of his story, Mr. Sterling stood, walked over to Damion, reached out, and shook his hand.

"You are a good man, Damion. Please take all the time you need. Believe me when I say your brother is very lucky to have you in his corner and vice versa."

Damion couldn't be more grateful. He pulled his hand out of Mr. Sterling's grip and hugged him. The twins had grown up without a father, and that's why Mr. Sterling's concern for him was touching. They had been surrounded by women all of their lives, and for the first time, Damion realized that he had missed out—not that he was complaining. Toni and Jaz had done the best they could. Still, there was a part of him that wished he knew his father. On several occasions he had asked his mother about his father, and her response was always the same.

"Damion, baby, your father was just a one-night stand. He doesn't know that he has sons. To be real, I wouldn't know where to begin if we decided to look for him."

However, Damion always had the feeling that his mother wasn't giving him the whole story.

Damion pulled away from Mr. Sterling, bent down to pick up his briefcase, and disappeared into the hall. Having become emotional, Damion did not want his boss to see the tears forming in his eyes.

Damion was going to take advantage of the free time. First thing he was going to do was to take a ride upstate.

* * * * *

Devon had arrived at the yard twenty minutes early. He needed time to think his plan through, and what better way than to walk the track. He checked out the surrounding area, looking for an escape out of the prison. Four years was enough time, and twenty-one more was a lifetime he wasn't willing to waste. The worst that could happen was he would get caught and get another seven years added to his sentence. Oh yeah, and disappoint everyone who loves him. That's a chance he would have to take, though.

Big Man arrived right on time. He knew Devon was stressed over his appeal, but he had never heard Devon speak the way he had that afternoon. Marcus also knew his friend well enough to know that he was up to no good. Marcus spotted Devon from across the football field.

"Yo, dawg, what's good? Why the grim look?" Marcus asked, approaching his boy.

"Ain't nothing, man. Just thinking."

"Alright, what's going on? You sounded as though this shit was a life or death situation?"

"It is. Before I start, let me get your word that no matter what happens this shit stays between us."

"Man, why you keep trying to play me? You know you can trust me. This must be some real serious shit," Marcus replied, while removing a pack of Newport 100's from his Army jacket.

Marcus and Devon began to walk slowly around the yard, when Devon suddenly turned and stood directly in front of Big Man.

"I need your help, man. I have a plan that will get me out of here."

"Okay, talk to me," Marcus responded, as he continued to smoke as though what Devon had said was nothing but a casual statement.

"Nah, Marcus, I don't think you understand what I'm saying."

"Alright, then make me understand."

"I have a plan that will get me out of here." Devon said, while looking at Marcus with extreme concentration.

"Yo, your ass is crazy, if you're thinking about what I think you're thinking!"

"Yo, lower your voice."

"I know you done lost your fuckin' mind for real now, Dee," Marcus continued, bringing it down a notch.

As they continued to walk, Devon filled him in on all the details. Although Marcus thought Devon's plan was farfetched, he agreed to be Devon's decoy.

Sexy

Chapter 5

"030606," the C.O. announced over the block's intercom.

"Yeah, what's up?" Devon hollered down to the C.O., who stood behind a bulletproof, knife-proof, anything-proof bubble.

"You got a visit."

"Thanks, man."

Devon wasn't expecting anyone, and no one usually showed up without letting him know first. The only person who would show up like that was Damion, Devon thought while brushing his teeth and scratching his balls, and if it was Damion, he couldn't have showed up at a better time.

Devon reached for his state greens and pulled them on. Then he slipped into a tan button-down shirt and laced his feet with a pair of tan construction Timbs. He took one last look in the mirror, then winked at his reflection. After seeing everything was in place, he headed towards the visiting room.

Damion walked through the metal detector and onto the visiting floor. After finding their assigned table, he headed to the vending machines and purchased everything he knew his brother liked to eat, along with a few extras.

"Yo, bro, who the fuck you feeding, an army?" Devon said, as he reached his brother and held his arms out.

Sexy

Damion just couldn't get used to seeing his brother in this fucked-up predicament. He couldn't begin to imagine how he lived day after day behind these walls.

"Nah, man, I haven't had lunch yet. I'm one hungry nigga. What's up with you? You hungry?" Damion asked, while standing and walking straight into his brother's arms.

They held each other for a few seconds, reassuring each other that they were not alone. Devon thought he was the one who had it bad, but he never really noticed just how much this shit was affecting Damion. He looked emotionally drained. It was definitely taking its toll.

"Hey, Dey, what's good? You alright, man?"

"Yeah, I'm good. What's up with you?"

"I'm good, son." Devon looked down at the table and motioned his twin to sit down. "I'm glad you showed up today. Waiting around all day to hear something about the appeal was getting to me. Thanks, bro. You always know when I need you."

"No problem. You know I always got your back," Damion stated, as he unwrapped a microwavable chicken and cheese sandwich.

"Yeah, I know. This is why I'm about to ask you something that's serious."

"Go ahead, ask. You already know that if you need anything, I got you. What's on your mind?"

"Well," Devon started, when suddenly his stomach began to twist. "I was thinking about getting out of here."

"Yeah, well, you know that's not going to be easy. It may be a few more years before anything goes through."

"Nah, Dey, you're not understanding me."

Devon reached out and took a hold of his brother's wrist as he was about to sling the rest of the sandwich into his mouth.

"Chill. Yo, what's wrong with you?" Damion said, then looked into his brother's eyes and recognized that look.

Devon was up to something, but what? Damion didn't want to ask out loud; however, curiosity got the best of him.

"What are you talkin' about? I know you got to be joking, right?"

"When do you ever know me to play around? I'm dead-ass serious," Devon replied.

"Oh, yeah, okay. So how the fuck do you plan on doing that? Ain't nobody ever in the history of New York State escaped from a max joint. Don't get me wrong. Many have tried, but were not successful. You're buggin'!"

"Ain't none of them achieved an escape, I give you that. But none of them had a twin brother either."

Devon was fully aware that his last words would get Damion's attention.

"What the fuck are you talkin' about, Dee? I know you don't think I'm going to give you the okay to do no dumb shit."

"I don't need your okay. All I need is your body."

"My body?"

"Chill, nigga. Lower your voice."

"My body?" Damion repeated in a whisper, looking deranged. "Are you on mental meds or something?"

"Dey, listen. Do you remember when we were kids and we used to play pranks on people by switching up? No one ever knew the difference."

"Yeah, Dee, but that's when we were kids, man. Are you trying to ask me to switch places with you in the P-Nile? You can't be serious, Dee."

"I ain't ever been more serious about anything. There is some unfinished business I need to take care of on the street. I already got the shit mapped out. All you have to do is say yes."

"Dee, just humor me for a minute. If I decided to go along with your insane scheme, how long would I have to be in here?"

"Just for seven days."

"Are you fuckin' crazy? Seven days?"

Damion couldn't believe what Devon had cooked up now. It was always some drama. But how could he deny his request? He owed his brother his life. Devon was in prison for protecting him. However, he had to put some thought into this. If they were to be discovered, they could both be sitting behind bars for the rest of their lives. With all of that in mind, he still needed and wanted to know Devon's plan.

The visit lasted three hours, during which time Damion made a conscious decision to release Devon's current attorney from his duties and hire someone else.

Damion was about to risk everything. His brother was talking crazy, but what could he really do to change his mind? Damion was far from convinced of his brother's plan. It sounded good, though.

Devon's vendetta towards Supreme was obsessive and ludicrous. He wasn't aware that Supreme was head of the black mafia now. They were a group of hustlers connected by kinship. He had recruited all of the men in his family, as well as a few young niggas in the community. Supreme's money was long, and had long gone to his head. From the day of Devon's arrest, Supreme blew up—leaving nothing to the imagination and leaving everyone else out on the streets high and dry. It had gotten to a point that there were several attempts on his life.

Damion took a back row seat and watched Supreme become untouchable. Supreme's dealing with drugs was not the only business he had invested in. His business had expanded. It included loan sharking, gambling, and prostitution. Supreme also had some of New York's finest on his payroll. Devon wouldn't be able to get within fifty feet of the target without being noticed, or worse murdered.

Damion had to find a way of erasing these crazy-ass thoughts from his brother's mind before he found himself behind bars for seven days.

Damion stepped onto the platform at the 125th Street Metro North Station. He hurried through, working his way towards the exit. He was so deep in thought that he hadn't realized he had just slammed straight into a young lady, knocking everything out of her hands. As she bent down to retrieve her belongings, she mumbled under her breath, making it difficult for him to understand what she was saying.

"Excuse me, miss. Are you okay?" Damion asked, while bending down to help her.

He wasn't expecting anything other than a sensible answer, but was surprised when the beautiful young lady began to curse his ass out.

"What, are you fuckin' blind? I can't believe this shit!"

"Miss, I said excuse me, or did you not hear me?"

Damion stood, handing her everything he was able to pick up from the ground.

"Well, you need to watch where the fuck you're going. A nigga could get hurt behind shit like this."

"Listen. I don't know who the fuck you think you're talking to, bitch. You act like I did this shit on purpose."

Heated, Damion pushed the items into her hand, turned around, and started to walk away. Venus looked on, feeling bad that she had gone off on the brother. She hadn't really taken a good look at him until now, and she found he looked good in his three-piece Ralph Lauren suit. She could tell the brother had class.

"Hey, stop! Listen. I'm sorry. I didn't mean to offend you."

Damion heard her calling after him, but chose to ignore her. Not having time for nobody's bullshit, he continued to walk toward the stairs that led to the corner of 125th Street and Park Avenue.

"Hey!" Venus yelled, as she ran behind him.

Damion turned slightly and saw her standing at the top of the steps wiping tears from her eyes. He wanted nothing more than to just get on with the rest of his day, but there was something about this chick that stopped him in his tracks.

"Yo, boo. It's alright, girl. Chill. Why are you crying? It's not that serious," Damion said to her, as he walked back up the steps to meet her.

Damion could hear his mother's voice in the back of his head. *Be a gentleman at all times.* Jaz had always told her sons to never treat a woman bad or disrespectfully. Women were the foundation of a man's life. Women should be treated like goddesses at all times, even when they didn't act like one.

By now, Damion was up on her, and she didn't look like no dragon. The tears alone showed him that there was a sensitive side to her. He reached for one of the bags she held in her hand and guided her down the steps.

"Listen. I'm sorry at the way I screamed at you back there. I'm on an emotional roller coaster, and I took it out on you. Please forgive me," Venus apologized, hoping this fine specimen of a man would look beyond her tough exterior.

Venus had just been released from prison. After serving fifteen years behind the walls, she had built a wall of her own. Time had hardened her heart, but not her soul. She knew when to admit she was wrong.

"So where are you headed?" Damion asked, as they reached the bottom of the steps.

Venus wasn't sure how to answer his question. She was afraid to let him know that she had just been released from Bedford Hills Correctional Facility. She didn't know how to explain that she was on her way to a homeless shelter.

"To be honest, I just need to find the Number Six train. Can you show me in which direction to go?"

"Sure. Follow me. I'll take you to the train station on Lexington Avenue. Then you are on your own."

"Cool!" Venus smiled as she walked alongside him.

Damion had noticed how she brushed the original question off. He also noticed the sparkle in her eyes—a shine he had never been aware of in any other woman. Damion kept looking down at her. She was cute, the way that she looked around as though she had never seen the area before. He found himself getting turned on by her sense of innocence. Damion especially liked how she said the word, "Cool." That was a turn-on in itself the way she formed her lips to sound out the word. The perfect shape outlined her mouth.

"Why are you looking at me like that? Do I have a foreign object on my face?"

"Nah. I hope you don't mind me saying this, but you are beautiful."

"Thanks," she replied, blushing at his compliment. "So are you."

"What are you doing tonight?" Devon asked, while holding her stare.

"I don't have any plans. Why?"

"Well, tonight is going to be your lucky night. Here is my business card. Call me when you get settled, and we'll hook up."

"Cool," she said again.

As she took the card from his hand, she felt an electrical shock run through her body.

This is going to be his lucky night, she thought, as she ran to catch the train that was heading towards the Lexington Avenue station.

Sexy

Chapter 6

Damion couldn't remember when he was last in the company of a beautiful woman. His whole world was centered on fighting Devon's defense. He needed time out for himself. He needed nothing more than to just lay back, relax, and hopefully get some pussy, too. Damion had neglected his needs long enough.

While standing on the corner trying to hail a cab, visions of Venus popped into his mind, and he wasn't surprised when his manhood became aroused. The mere thought of her brought his body to life. Venus was in for the time of her life.

Before he entered the Woolworth Building on Broadway, where he was to meet with Trouble's attorney, he stopped off at a nearby CVS store to purchase a box of condoms and a pack of Newport 100's. Maybe he was getting ahead of himself, but it was better to be safe than sorry.

* * * * *

Venus had no idea what she was going to wear. She was excited. Who would have thought that on her first day back on the street, she would have met a potential boyfriend? Venus searched in her bag for the card Damion had given her. She noticed the quality of the paper on which his information was printed was not cheap. She also noticed in big, bold letters the address where he worked: WALL STREET.

"Damn, I hit the jackpot," she softly whispered to herself.

This was an once-in-a-lifetime opportunity to get her groove back, like Stella. She was going to make this a night to remember. He would be hooked, but first she had to pay her parole officer a visit.

When the train came to a complete stop at the Port Authority station, she quickly placed Damion's business card back into her bag, jumped up, and ran off the train. Standing in the middle of the mass confusion New Yorkers found themselves in every day, Venus felt like a tourist. The Port Authority looked completely different from when she last saw it because they had made some major renovations.

Finally arriving in front of the parole building, she walked in and found herself face to face with half a dozen convicts trying to do exactly what she was doing…reporting. She approached the front desk, gave her name, and then waited to be instructed on what to do next.

"It will be one hour or so before your name is called. You can find a seat in the waiting area."

"Thanks," Venus said, while turning to look for an empty chair.

There were none available. The fellas sitting there had their heads buried in newspapers, making pen marks in the Want Ads, as if they were really looking for a job.

"Where are all the gentlemen of the world today," she stated, as she coughed out loud, trying to get their attention. *Not in here,* she guessed because she was being ignored.

Venus wasn't looking her best yet, but damn, these niggas were straight-up, low-class derelicts. She decided to just stand against a wall and wait. Once she finished with her parole officer, she would go shopping and get everything she needed to make her appearance much more desirable.

At the present moment, she was living on a tight budget, and would have to work with what she had. Venus was determined to find something alluring, yet inexpensive. She needed to find something to blow her man's mind. *Her man* is how she referred to him, because she was taught in prison by the old-timers to claim what you know deep in your heart is yours—or about to be.

As Venus quietly stood against the wall checking out her surroundings, something twisted in her mind—the negative side of her situation. It just suddenly crept up on her. Damion wasn't under any circumstances going to accept a woman who had just completed a 15-year bid. He didn't seem the thuggish type, and from his business card, he was a man of higher education, although the time for Venus had not been wasted.

During her stay at Bedford Hills Correctional, Venus had obtained her G.E.D. and then went on to college, where she earned her Master's degree in Human Behavior. Thoughts on how to begin to tell him her story made her feel inferior.

When Venus finished reporting, she left the parole building in better spirits than when she first walked in. Mr. Jackson, Venus's parole officer, had given her a list of job openings. He knew her history and educational background, so he had taken it upon himself to say a few words of reassurance. He had also taken the time out to search the internet to form a list of jobs for which he knew she had the qualifications.

From the moment he opened her file, Mr. Jackson felt she had received a bum rap, and because of his spirituality, he believed in second chances. Suddenly, her world seemed a little brighter.

Venus quickened her step, bumping into pedestrians and excusing herself along the way. Fighting traffic was another difficult task, as well. New York City had a life of its own.

Sexy

This is going to take some getting used to, she thought.

Now standing on the corner of 57th Street and Fifth Avenue, she searched for a women's clothing store—a place where she could get in touch with the woman who was desperately trying to emerge. Venus had been sent to prison at a very young age, and had grown up with a population of women who came from different backgrounds. She always tried to maintain her own style—an untouchable sense of uniqueness, something she could call her own. Venus had always been capable of holding it down, but now in the free world, she was about to get loose. She wanted to find something exotic and sexy. Her goal was to capture Damion's heart and leave him breathless at first sight.

Venus walked into Victoria's Secret, where she picked out a panty and bra set from their Angel Collection. She felt like a little girl in a candy store. There was so much to choose from. As she walked away from the counter with a pink and black shopping bag, she promised herself that she would return one day to purchase every single item.

Next, she walked over to Madison Avenue, where all of the biggest names in the fashion industry were located—Gucci, Prada, Louis Vuitton, Tommy Hilfiger, etc., etc. You name it, those designers had their spot.

She glanced at the windows and noticed there were no price tags visible. Venus thought back to the nights she spent in her cell admiring the clothing shown to her in magazines. She never once stopped daydreaming of the day when she would be able to shop at these same stores where she now stood. With her funds were running low, she would never be able to get exactly what she wanted, but she continued to look through the window of the Gucci boutique anyway.

She held her composure when she sensed that someone was looking at her a little too hard. Immediately, she turned to her right and caught a shadow from inside the store. Venus leaned closer to the glass and came face to face with the sales clerk. The young woman looked directly into

Venus's eyes and saw that she was troubled by something. Brenda walked over to the door, stuck her head out, and motioned to Venus to enter the store. Venus was embarrassed. She didn't realize she had been standing outside the store for several minutes daydreaming.

"Hi!" Brenda said, as she waved her hand in front of Venus's eyes. "Are you alright? I noticed you standing out there with a blank look on your face."

Brenda was now escorting Venus to a lounge area.

"Yeah, I'm fine. I was just admiring your window display."

"Well, did you see something you like?"

Venus nodded her head up and down, as she politely sat down and placed her bags to the right of her feet.

"We have a huge selection of different designs. What did you have in mind?"

"Well, I have a date tonight. I would like to wear something sexy, yet ghetto'fied."

Venus smiled at her last remark. She had come across that word in one of the many urban tales she had read while incarcerated.

Brenda smiled because she knew exactly what she meant, and was already pulling clothing off the racks.

"Okay, let me see, girl. Stand up. What size are you? A 5/6 or 7/8?"

"I'm not sure," Venus replied, while holding her hands to her waist.

"Why don't we step over here to the dressing room? You can try on these items first. Don't worry, girl. We will find something for your date."

Venus thanked her as she stepped behind the door.

In hopes of making a sale, Brenda continuously passed blouses, dresses, slacks, and skirts to her. Little did she know that Venus didn't have a pot to piss in or a window to throw it out of. She didn't have to know. Besides, who was going to tell her? Venus sure wasn't. She was too busy having fun trying on all of the different silks and cashmeres.

Temptation got the better of her, though. She tried to fight it for as long as she could, but Venus had to do what she had to do. She slipped a black, silk, low-cut mini-dress into her small handbag, and prayed Brenda wouldn't notice. Hopefully, she hadn't kept track of all the items she had handed to her. It was a chance she was willing to take, though. So not to look suspicious, Venus would purchase something—a small item, something that wouldn't hurt her pockets.

Venus walked out of the dressing room fully dressed in her own gear, leaving everything else behind, and informed the sales clerk of her disapproval. "Nothing fit right."

She then approached the checkout counter and asked Brenda to show her one of the many pair of sunglasses that sat inside the glass case. After she had selected the right pair for the shape of her face, they walked over to the register, where Brenda rang the price of the item.

"That will be two hundred and fifty dollars. Will that be cash or credit?"

"Cash," Venus said, while digging for her wallet.

Brenda recognized a thief when she saw one. Having been trained by security on what to look out for, the woman before her displayed all the signs. She was nervous and in a hurry. Brenda watched her carefully now, as well as when she was behind the dressing room door. Brenda was far from stupid.

When Brenda handed Venus back her change from the three hundred dollars, she grabbed her wrist. Venus looked horrified as she scrambled backwards. After pulling her arm back, breaking Brenda's grip, she began to walk quickly towards the exit. Brenda jumped over the counter like Cat Woman and landed directly on top of Venus, pinning her to the floor with her body.

"Your biggest mistake was opening your purse and giving me full view of what you had inside," Brenda said, while grabbing for Venus's bag.

"Yo, what the fuck are you doing?" Venus screamed, trying to get Brenda off of her.

"Shut the fuck up before I call the police," Brenda shouted into Venus's ear, as she wrestled for the bag.

"Call the police for what, you stupid bitch? Get the fuck off of me."

Now the shit was really going to hit the fan. If her P.O. was notified of her petty larceny attempt, she would be sent back to prison. She had to think and think fast.

"Okay, okay, chill. Please don't call the cops. Just get off of me and let me explain."

"No. First, give me the dress, and then we can talk."

Venus found it best just to hand over the bag, and then maybe Brenda wouldn't call the police. Maybe she would just take the dress back and let Venus go without a second thought. So, she handed Brenda the bag as they both lifted themselves off the floor.

"Listen, please. Let me explain."

"Explain what? Are you nuts? What are you trying to do, make me lose my job?"

"Nah, girl."

"Well, I don't want to hear your sorry-ass excuses. Why don't you go out and look for a job like everyone else?"

Brenda removed the dress, which was worth twenty-five hundred dollars, from the bag. The dress was screaming sex appeal. Brenda had been working for Gucci for over two years and still couldn't afford to buy one of their dresses. Maybe listening to Venus wouldn't be such a bad idea.

Sexy

Chapter 7

Devon wasn't too thrilled about having to wait for his next visit. The days would seem so much longer now. That's when Damion would let him know if the plan was a go-ahead. He had heard Damion out when they discussed who Supreme was today. A lot had changed in four years, but what Damion didn't know was that Devon was well informed on Supreme. He knew exactly what he was up against. Soldiers from the hood walked in and out of the penitentiary on a daily basis, and they would inform Devon of Supreme's criminal activities in exchange for small favors.

Supreme had no idea the chaos that was about to interrupt his world. That's exactly how Devon wanted it to be. Devon wanted to catch Supreme when he least expected it. He would creep up on him like a thief in the night. When he was most vulnerable, Devon would get him.

Yes, it was a known fact that things had changed in the last four years. But one thing for sure and two things for certain, Supreme hadn't changed. No one knew Supreme quite like Devon did. He knew his strengths, his weaknesses, and most of all, he knew his fears. Devon had learned early on that if he was going to survive in the game he would have to learn how to read the other players. He had become a whiz at the challenge. This is why he found it strange that one of the waitresses at Club Ecstasy was unable to handle an uninvited guest.

All of the employees, from dancers to cocktail waitresses, had been interviewed thoroughly. They were also screened for past associations. If hired, they were trained by Chyna personally. Aside from serving the customers, their job was to handle any situation that arose within the establishment. So, something just didn't seem right.

It had never dawned on him until this very moment that chick was down with it. Supreme must have paid her off to get him to the door. Devon couldn't put his finger on it, but part of his plan was to find out what exactly was supposed to have gone down that night. He hoped that Chyna didn't get rid of the girl. He definitely needed to get to her.

As an afterthought, Devon hurried out onto the tier, and walked with long strides out of the block. With his hands in his pockets and his head hung low, flashes of gunfire came into play. He felt like a caged animal. Needing to touch base with Marcus, he headed towards the yard. There he could clear his mind, talk to Marcus, and finalize the details of his escape.

He walked through a gate, showed his State I.D., and waited. When his entrance was approved by the C.O., he immediately began to feel uncomfortable. Devon brushed it off, thinking that maybe his nerves were getting the best of him since he had a lot on his plate.

Devon waited over by the weights area. He searched for Marcus, but he was nowhere to be found. Devon noticed a bunch of young thugs glaring at him, as if they wanted to do something to him. Now was not the time to get into any bullshit-ass altercations, so he brushed that shit off, too. He walked to the outfield by the track, and circled around the track twice before he was struck on the right side of his face, which caused him to lose his balance slightly.

TWOFOLD

Devon could not believe he was struck by one of the chump-ass niggas. He didn't know them and didn't want to know them, so why? Who cared? In prison, niggas didn't need a reason, and you didn't ask questions. It was considered a sign of weakness.

Devon found himself in a squat position, as he waited for their next move. While his eyes analyzed the situation, he realized he wasn't just dealing with one person. There were four sets of Timbs surrounding him. Now shit was about to get cranked up.

He looked for the brotha with the biggest feet. That was the one that would have to be brought down first. The others would just have to wait their turn. Devon, who had to fight his whole young life to protect what belonged to him, was good with his hands. He loved the techniques in street fighting, but he was most intrigued by the boxing matches he watched on TV while growing up.

Encouraged by his mother to join the Boys & Girls Club on 111th Street in Spanish Harlem, Devon had been able to enhance his boxing skills. With 20 knockouts and 0 losses, Devon was asked by his trainer to join the Golden Glove Championships at Madison Square Garden. Unfortunately, his life had taken a different course, and he denied the request.

Now with four niggas standing above him, he had to think fast. He reached out for the size 12 shoes, grabbed his opponent by the ankles, and pulled as hard as his arms permitted him. Devon watched as he fell to the ground and screamed, "Oh, shit!" The kid looked terrorized. It had been a surprise attack, a move he wasn't ready for.

The sound that escaped from Devon's mouth was that of a mountain lion. Devon leaped up and landed directly on top of the kid. Blow for blow, Devon fought, never giving the kid a chance to connect. It was over before it even began.

His partners in the background stood in a semicircle. The guard at the tower turned his back, thinking it was just

55

another gang related meeting. He was used to those. Usually they didn't become violent, so he just turned around and looked the other way.

Out of nowhere, Devon felt the pressure as someone tossed him to the side and on his ass, ripping away his shirt. Blood was everywhere on his hands, face, and white wife beater. From a distance, he heard what sounded like bones cracking. Devon wanted to know who the hell was causing these bones to be disfigured. So, he sat up, leaning on his elbow for support. Before he was half sitting up, he heard Marcus's voice.

"Get up, you punk-ass bitch," Marcus sang, hollered, and yelled.

It didn't matter how he said it; all of it sounded like music to Devon's ears.

"I said, get up. I don't want to have to dislocate your face, son."

Devon was not looking forward to spending any time in the box. He had other things he needed to do. He had to find a way of bringing all of this shit to an end. General Population is where he needed to be in order for his plan to work. Devon thought about all of this as he tried to stand up, but couldn't. His head was spinning out of control.

Word got around fast behind the walls. It struck Marcus as kind of odd that Devon was about to be jumped out in the yard. Devon wasn't the type of nigga to get into any beef. None of these riff-raffs were worth spending one or two years locked down—confined to a small cell with only bare walls to look at and a steel bed to rest your restless body on. After listening to the gossip that circulated around the block, Marcus decided to check things out for himself. He couldn't just go by mere hearsay.

"Yo, what's really good, Dee? You alright, man?" Marcus asked, as he reached for Devon's hand and pulled him to his feet.

"Yeah, man," he said to his boy. "What the fuck is going on?" he yelled at the figure that lay on the ground.

Devon suddenly snapped. He looked at each one square in the face, taking deep breaths to gain some of his senses. That's when he realized he was looking at a bunch of young kids—all under the age of twenty-one.

There had been rumors that this group was considered hired help within the walls—hired to take care of a nigga's dirty work. They came cheap, too.

"How much?" Devon barked, while gritting his teeth.

Luc, Cat, and Al-B looked at each other as though they had no idea what Devon was talking about. Devon moved in closer, gripped Al-B's cheeks, and squeezed them together as hard as he could.

"Answer me, motherfucker! How much did they pay your sorry ass to get at me?"

"Don't say shit, man. Ya'll know what time it is."

The voice came from Toy, who was still laid back in the cut. Although hurt from Devon's beat down, he was still talking shit. Marcus grabbed Toy by the throat, tightening his grip as he made his next statement.

"Oh, so you're the leader of the pack, ha! Well, since you want to be a hero, let me do you off first."

Marcus continued to apply pressure on his esophagus, causing his eyes to roll back into his head. When he felt the kid had enough, he released his grip, and then asked the same question.

"How much? And while you're at it, give me the name of your employer."

"You know better than that. I'll be a dead man if I snitch on these people," Toy choked with each word that escaped his mouth.

"You'll be a dead man anyway, so you ain't saying nothing, slick."

Devon stood stone-faced, watching as Marcus grabbed for Toy's neck again.

"Chill, man. We ain't going to get nowhere if you choke his ass to death," Devon finally said. He needed answers, not another state bid.

Toy was struck by fear. He was in a fucked-up predicament. When he was first approached with this job offer, he was not well informed on Devon's ways. He was not the one to fuck with. Toy was not told that Devon had a partner he needed to look out for. He hadn't asked any questions either. Fifty thousand dollars split four ways was enough to take the job, no questions asked. Lack of financial stability caused him not to get all the information he needed to accomplish the job successfully. His portion of the money was going to be a step up for him. Toy thought that with his share of the money he would be able to start something sweet once he hit the streets. Now, he wasn't sure.

His life would depend on the choices he made at the present moment. With thirty days left on his sentence, he was capable of singing like a bird. Toy wasn't sure if it was worth all of the bullshit he was going through.

"Alright, check it. Let my niggas go and I'll talk to you."

Cat and Al-B turned away quickly. They were ready to walk, pulling Luc by the arm. Al-B looked back at Toy; he needed to know that Toy knew what he was doing. There was a certain loyalty between them.

When Toy motioned for him to leave, Al-B asked him, "Yo, nigga, you sure this is what you want to do?"

"Yea, Bee. I'm good. Just keep your mouth shut."

"Alright, dawg. Keep your head up."

Al-B walked off, knowing there was a good chance he would never see his boy alive again.

Chapter 8

Venus stood in front of a full-length mirror located on the back of Brenda's bedroom door.

"Damn, girl, this dress looks good on me," Venus said, as she looked at herself from behind.

The booty was tight, thighs were banging, and tits, well, they were firm and just right. Not too big and not too small. Perfect. They say that more than a mouth full is a waste. She had it all in all the right places. What a blessing!

Brenda pushed the door open, almost knocking Venus aside. She was holding two full glasses of Alizé, and displaying a look of admiration. She had to admit the dress was a big hit. Absolutely gorgeous.

"You are definitely saying something in that dress, girl. Here, let's get our drink on before you go out on this date."

"Babbyyy, I'ma hurt somebody tonight."

The ladies giggled as they clicked their glasses together, toasting to their newfound friendship. Suddenly, they both fell silent. Venus, in a shaky tone, tried to express to Brenda her deepest gratitude. Back at the boutique, Brenda had given her the chance to explain her situation. She listened without judgment, something most people would never do.

Venus didn't have many friends behind the wall, and she had even fewer on the streets. All of that was about to change, though.

After several hours of doing the girl thing—hair, manicures, and pedicures—Venus was impressed with the final results.

"Yo, Vee, you look like you just walked off the cover of Vibe Magazine."

"Thanks. If it wasn't for you, I don't know how I would have pulled it off. Did I thank you?"

"Yeah, for the millionth time, so stop it. It was my pleasure helping a sistah out. You know we have to stick together when times are hard." Brenda rolled her eyes then sat on her queen size bed.

"I feel you. You were heaven sent."

"Yeah, I know. Now get the rest of your stuff on before you're late?"

Brenda reached for the Gucci shades Venus had purchased, along with a handbag they borrowed from the store. The outfit was now complete.

"Perfect," Brenda purred like a cat.

"It is, isn't it?" Venus said, while heading for the door.

"Listen, Vee. Here, use these tonight. I don't want you waking me out of my beauty sleep."

Venus turned around to find Brenda standing with her arm stretched out, holding a set of keys in her hand. Venus stood there frozen, looking confused. For starters, she had not held a set of keys in years. Secondly, she felt overwhelmed that Brenda had opened up her heart as well as her home. Venus didn't know what to say to her.

Brenda had tried her damndest to keep her feelings in her pocket as she heard Venus's story. Brenda had grown up in one of the toughest parts of East Harlem. She had watched as her people lost themselves to the streets. Some made it out, while some didn't. Many of them sat in the P-Nile now. This is why she had asked Venus to stay with her until she was able to get a place of her own. There was easiness about Venus she couldn't ignore. All Venus needed was a break—someone to lend her a helping hand.

"Here, girl. Stop looking at me like I got two heads. I have things to do."

As Brenda shook the keys at Venus with force, Venus walked back toward Brenda to ask her if she was sure it was okay.

"Of course, it's okay. I ain't getting up to get no door. I have a life, you know."

A smile spread across Brenda's lips, as she opened Venus's hand and placed the keys directly in her palm. Then she closed her fingers into a fist.

"Now go have fun, and don't be giving it up on the first date. You want the brotha to come back."

"Yeah, I know, but I can't promise you anything. It's been a long time."

They both smiled at each other. That moment had meant a lot to Venus. Brenda's trust in her was a step up from what she was used to.

"See you in the morning," Venus said, and then left out the door.

Venus found herself on the corner of 96th Street and Lexington Avenue, heading toward Fifth Avenue where Damion was supposed to pick her up. Damion had mentioned during their brief conversation some places where they could head out to. However, they never decided on one set place. Tonight was going to be a surprise for the both of them. Venus wanted to just go with the flow. Whatever he had decided to do was okay with her.

Damion purchased two tickets on the Cruise to Nowhere—an exclusive yacht that drifted up the Hudson River, and then down again. There they would dine, dance, and enjoy a laidback atmosphere. This was something he could really get into, especially in light of his brother's crazy plan. There was nothing he needed more than to just relax.

He also wanted to show Venus her worth. After being in prison so many years, Venus deserved to be showered with the finest things. She needed to experience a new way of life.

That afternoon, Damion had asked the new attorneys working on Devon's case to run a background check on Venus. He understood plainly how corny that was, but one couldn't be too careful, though. He couldn't take any chances. Times had changed. It was easy to mistaken sneakiness for a sense of innocence. His life was filled with doubts, so he was taking precautions. Damion had to make sure he wasn't about to deal with no psycho bitch.

After receiving the written report he had requested, he felt a little disappointed. Her past was staring him in the face as he read word for word that she had been incarcerated for murder. That wasn't going to stop him from getting to know her better, though. There was something about her that held his interest. It was a chance he was willing to take.

He personally could not imagine life locked down, but he was about to find out. At this time next week, he would be 030606, a convicted felon. Maybe the experience would make him a better man.

As he crossed the Triboro Bridge, he popped his Usher CD into the player, turned up the volume, and pushed his seat back slightly. Finally arriving at his destination, he looked up the street to Fifth Avenue, and there on the southwest corner was an unavoidable sight. He was amazed at how beautiful Venus appeared from a distance. As he slowly turned onto the avenue, it was plain to see that she was more than just beautiful. Venus was gorgeous. Exotic was more the word he was looking for. Damion pulled his Lexus up to the curb, cracking the window a little so she wouldn't be startled.

"What's up, baby girl. You ready for the time of your life?"

Venus was immediately in a trance. Her eyes became low and transparent. All of her feelings were held behind her soft brown eyes.

Damn, what a sight for sore eyes is all she thought of at that moment. How was she to survive staring into that face all night? The brotha looked good in his white linen suit. The soft fabric looked delicious against his year-round tan. What affected her most were his cat-shaped eyes and their color— so different from what she had ever seen. That is what made him all the more alluring.

Venus was awakened by his sudden movement. He had been standing there holding the passenger door open. *What a gentleman,* she thought.

"Yes, I'm ready. The question is, are you ready?" she asked playfully, her smile brightening all of 96th Street. She continued on to say, "I have been ready for this all of my life."

"Don't worry, baby. I'ma make this night one you'll never forget."

"I'm counting on that."

Venus walked past him and stepped up into the truck, exposing her long shapely legs. When she was safely secured by the seatbelt, only then was he able to breathe. Venus was without a doubt breathtaking and intoxicating.

Pier 52 off the Westside Highway was up ahead. As they approached the ramp leading up to the yacht, Venus stopped short. Her legs became heavy. She felt as though her legs had been weighed down by cement blocks. She couldn't believe her eyes. Venus had never seen anything more beautiful. The lights outlining the ship were soft and inviting. The music was seductively smooth with a calming effect, and yet it held an upbeat tempo. The couples ascending to the yacht wore not only designer suits and dresses, but also wore their class and elegance as easily as they wore hood gear.

"Oh my God!"

Sexy

"What's wrong, Venus? Are you alright?" Damion asked, as he wrapped his arms around her waist.

"Oh my God!" Venus repeated, while leaning back into his embrace.

"You already said that. Is there something wrong?"

"No, Damion, nothing's wrong. Everything is perfect...absolutely perfect."

Chapter 9

Once away from unwelcome ears, Toy analyzed his situation. There weren't many choices. He thought it would be wise to give Devon and Marcus the information, and hopefully, they would spare his life. The plan was to kill Devon. How he did it was left to his discretion. The hit man didn't ask for anything special, like torture. His only order was "make it clean". It seemed pretty easy at the time, and of course, the money gained was going into something useful.

Toy had watched Devon for several days, getting his routine down pat. This was supposed to make the hit all the easier. While he watched, Toy's boys were making the shank he planned on using. Devon wasn't supposed to get out of the yard alive. Fortunately for him, Marcus had been on point.

It didn't come as a surprise that Supreme's name was mentioned several times during the course of their meeting. Devon was not big on recruiting soldiers; however, now was the time to start—not so much for himself, since hopefully he would be out of there soon. It was his brother he was worried about. It would be déjà vu if they went after Damion again, thinking it was him. He had to clear this mess up before he could even consider switching with Damion.

"Yo, check it. Give me a minute with my man. Stand over there. Don't fuckin' move either," Devon told him as he squared off in his face.

Devon and Marcus moved over to the side. What they had to discuss was confidential.

"What's up, kid? What you want to do?" Marcus asked.

Marcus was ready for anything to jump off. All Devon had to do was give him the word.

"Big Man, now is the time to get some of these little niggas over to our side—whatever the price, money talks and bullshit walks."

"Yeah, so what's good?" Marcus suddenly lowered himself into a squatting position.

"Toy is about to get released, right?"

"Yeah."

"I'ma need this nigga on the outside, right?"

"Yo, why don't you just get to the motherfuckin' point? Dee, I'm not in the mood to play fifty questions with you. Stop playin' fuckin' head games."

"Chill, man. I'm about to tell you. I was thinking I could use this clown to get me closer to Supreme. He already got one foot in the door."

Marcus smiled at the idea, knowing damn well where Devon was going with this.

"So what you saying, dawg? Give it to me raw. What you want to do?"

"Okay, check it. I'ma tell him that he is to go directly to Damion upon his release. Dey would be the one to hit him off with the cheddar I'm about to offer him for his services. I'ma make it seem like his information was worth more than fifty G's."

"Oh, shit. Yo, that's why you my man. I like the way you think. He is going to think that he is going to meet your brother, but in all reality, you're really leading him to you."

"So what you think?"

"I think you is one smart nigga. The only thing that I'm worried about is if your brother is really going to come through."

"Yeah, he just needs a little time to let the idea sink in."

"Alright, man, you know him better than anyone."

Devon began to execute the plan as they walked back to where Toy was standing.

"Yo, why you smoking that rollie? Here, throw that shit out," Devon said, then dug into his pocket, pulled out a fresh pack of Newports, and handed one over to Toy.

Toy was not able to hear a word of Devon and Marcus's brief conversation. His nerves were on edge. Rollies, Newports—it didn't matter what he was smoking. He needed something to ease his mind. Devon's gesture was a sure sign that he was in the clear. Hopefully, Devon wouldn't look at his betrayal as negative. Toy needed them just as much as they needed him, or so he thought.

Devon was far from stupid. He knew exactly what Toy was thinking. He stared him in his eyes; all signs of panic had vanished. Devon thought about how stupid this kid really was. Toy really believed he could get away with the underhanded shit he had just pulled. Toy had just broken one of the main codes of the streets. He might have broken more than one, but he was too stupid to realize it. One thing for sure, Devon planned on using him and then ridding him of his own misery. Devon had to respect him, though, for at least trying to save his own ass. Too bad he played himself; the little nigga had potential.

Toy ditched the cigarette and waited for Devon to speak. He wanted Devon to stop clocking him. If he was going to do something, he wanted it over with. The anticipation was getting to him.

"What's up, son?" Toy asked, standing firm in his position. Whatever was whatever.

To his amazement, Devon cracked a smile—the kind that would run chills up and down your spine. Nevertheless, they were about to establish some type of communication.

"Everything is everything, boy," Marcus responded, while sliding up behind Toy.

Devon began to tell Toy what it was he wanted from him. After Devon relayed his instructions, Toy walked away.

"Yo, Big Man, make sure you keep an eye on him. That nigga can't be trusted."

"I got you, Dee."

* * * * *

"There is nothing like smoking some potent hydro to ease your mind," Supreme said, before taking a pull on the neatly rolled cigar his boy Twista had just finished packing.

His adrenaline was on overdrive, and he needed something to relax. Dealing with unsavory characters was not in his nature, but what choice did he have.

Toy had come highly recommended, although he sat patiently waiting for news on his order. It was said that no news was good news. Getting someone on the inside willing to get rid of Devon was not a problem. Fifty thousand dollars was a lot of money in the joint. He probably could have gotten the job done for less, but why take the chance. Supreme had to offer an amount that couldn't be refused. He was the type of brotha that was used to getting his way. The word NO was not part of his vocabulary. Supreme had become accustomed to being served hand and foot because of his status in the hood. People catered to his every need, and he held the power of control in his hands. Even now, as he sat among his surroundings—his home, his safety net—he realized that his life was being governed by the streets.

Thanks to the crackheads that showed their loyalty on a daily basis, Supreme was able to purchase a three-story brownstone located on 117th Street between First Avenue and Pleasant. For years, the building had been abandoned, but with the help of some fellows out of Brooklyn, he was able to restore its natural structure. He had taken the time to design the interior of his home using his lifestyle as the foundation.

Only he knew the secrets that lay behind the walls. The few that were hired to build his little secrets had been eliminated for security reasons. He wasn't willing to risk his safety because of some minor setbacks.

Since the day that Devon had crossed him, he was unable to trust anyone. Supreme had taken him under his wing and showed him everything he knew about the business, only to later find out that Devon had betrayed him. For that, he would pay.

For years, Supreme had been looking for ways to remove Devon from this earth—a way that would never lead back to him. Devon had a lot of people who would risk everything to retaliate, especially his Uncle Lizard who had Washington Height on lockdown. The Geechies weren't nothing to play with either. Let's not forget his mother, Jaz, a true gangster to the heart. He could remember the story of the Central Park slaying of this young kid who had snitched on her people.

His thoughts were suddenly interrupted by the sound of the ringing phone. The call that he was waiting for was finally coming through, with good news, he hoped.

"Yeah, talk to me." Supreme leaned back in his chair, while extending his legs, resting them on his cherry-colored mahogany desk.

"It's been taken care of," the voice said from the other end.

"Good. I'll take care of you. Come see me when you get out."

"A'ight, man. One."

"One."

Supreme rested the phone back on its cradle. Reaching over his desk, he looked at Twista and said, "Get the car ready. We got to make this run."

Twista nodded and then headed for the French doors, which separated the rooms. Twista was one of the few able to get close to Supreme. Because Twista had proven his loyalty, along with his effective ways of dealing with the game, Supreme allowed him some admittance. But not too far from Supreme's mind were his suspicions. Devon's actions had made it bad for the next nigga.

Supreme couldn't believe it was finally over. Devon had cost him plenty. He would never cross another brotha. Supreme's only regret was not being there to watch Devon take his last breath. Other than that, there was no love lost. Supreme felt no sympathy for Devon or his people. Fuck them if they couldn't take a joke.

Chapter 10

Venus climbed the ramp that led to the entrance of the dining cruise yacht. She glided through the door with her smooth and easy moves, as though she were the queen of some foreign country. As her eyes widened at the scenery, her heart opened up to looking at Damion, who stood closely at her side. She thanked all of the gods for sending her an angel. Venus loved the way he knew exactly what it was that she needed. The closest she had ever come to a dining hall was at Bedford Hills Correctional Facility—a memory she wanted nothing more than to forget. This picture was beyond anything she had ever seen. She wanted so badly to erase the last fifteen years of her life.

They were ushered to their reserved table by the yacht's host. While walking, Venus noticed the lights were turned down low, giving the place a romantic atmosphere. The stunning couples' shadows danced with each flicker of the candles that were placed as centerpieces. The gold crown moldings and high ceilings confirmed that this was going to be a night of elegance.

Damion held the small of her back, as they reached the cozy little corner made for two. He could feel the excitement flow through her body. Once at their table, he gently guided her onto her seat. After sitting down directly across from her, he began to pay her compliments.

"Venus, you look gorgeous tonight."

"Thank you. You look gorgeous, too. This place is amazing."

There was no ignoring the view, especially the one before her.

"I had a feeling you would like it."

"Well, you were right. I can't believe it," Venus said.

"All for you, baby."

Damion was putting Venus to the test by flattering her. He needed to see what she was all about. Would she share her past with him? He wanted her to feel comfortable enough to give one hundred percent with no limits. They were so enthralled with each other that neither noticed their waitress approach the table.

Samantha introduced herself, and then began to tell them the evening's specials. Elegantly dressed in a black and white tuxedo, black pumps, and a black bowtie, she looked like she belonged on Victoria's Secret's runway, not serving food on a yacht. Then again, this was New York City. Many of the model types took odd jobs until they landed their dream.

They ordered their first round of drinks, cognac for him and white wine for her. As soon as the waitress walked away, Damion continued down the path he had been going.

"So, young lady, tell me about yourself."

"What would you like to know?"

"Everything. I want to know your likes and dislikes, your wants and your needs. What makes such a beautiful woman like you find this place so different from any place else?"

Damion had set the bait. Now it was up to Venus to bite. Venus became nervous. How was she going to explain her excitement to this man without putting herself on the cross? Venus wanted to begin their friendship by being honest. Besides, what's the worst that could happen? Damion could

72

either walk away after hearing the truth, never to see her again, or he could be understanding and fall madly in love. Venus would have to accept either-or. She could always move on and explore other avenues. There were too many men out there looking for a chick like her, one that could be a lady in the streets and a freak in the sheets. Then again, why not just be honest? She had nothing to lose and much to gain.

Venus leaned forward, motioning him to lean in closer, too. She didn't want anyone else to hear what she had to say.

"Damion, I need to be honest with you as well as with myself. I find this place different because I have never had the privilege of coming to a place like this."

"What do you mean by you've never been to a place like this. I'm sure you have dated, right? What did those other brothers do? Take you to Mickey D's?" he queried with a smirk on his face.

"No, Damion." Venus hesitated for a minute, thinking that maybe telling Damion the truth wouldn't be such a good idea. Venus took a deep breath and continued. "Damion, I was away for a long time," Venus whispered, praying he would read in between the lines.

"Away? Away where?"

"Shhhh, lower your voice. Listen, Damion, I was in prison."

There she had walked through the lion's den. There was no turning back now because she knew his next question would be why. It was no mystery that she would have to explain her past situation. Now all she had to do was wait for his response.

Be it negative or positive, she had to admit it was as if a ton of bricks had been lifted off her shoulders. Venus had to come to terms with the truth and so did society. Society would have to accept her for who she was today, not judge her on her past. The felony conviction would always be a part of her. However, Venus was not ashamed of what she had done. Venus had to do what she had done to be the woman she was today. It was her destiny.

Venus searched in Damion's eyes for some sign of rejection. Damion searched in Venus's eyes for some sign of relief. He had never been in her position, but he could imagine how she must have felt. The moment of truth had arrived.

"How long were you away?"

"Fifteen years."

"Damn, baby. That was a long time. If you don't mind my asking, what happened?"

Before he was able to continue with the fifty questions, Venus said, "Listen. I don't mean to be rude or anything, but I really don't want to ruin our evening by discussing my past. With time, you will get to know my story."

Venus had become somewhat defensive, yet she said what was on her mind. It wouldn't have been Venus if she hadn't.

* * * * *

The last fifteen years had been a nightmare. At the tender age of sixteen, Venus had been the daughter of a heroin addict, and a mother to her two-year-old daughter and two younger siblings. She was a wife to a small-time drug pusher in the South Bronx. Venus had taken responsibility for everyone in her life, all the while forgetting about herself. Having to take care of her younger siblings had cost her own childhood. She cooked, cleaned, and changed diapers while her mother ran the streets.

The evening she was arrested for murder in the second degree, Venus had been hurrying home from the supermarket, struggling to make it back on time to make dinner for the little ones. Thank God for one of her neighbors, who on occasion lent a helping hand. If not for Ms. Summers, she would have had to lug the pack along with her. Just two steps from her apartment building, Venus heard a woman crying out for help. She would have kept going; it was only natural in the hood for women to beg for mercy. Since nine times out of ten their abusers were their husbands, boyfriends, or baby daddies, no one usually got involved. Something nagged at her, though. The cry was familiar. When she realized it was her mother's voice that penetrated her senses, she headed into the alley.

Venus saw two figures in the shadows. One was lying on the floor screaming, and another standing over her, kicking, punching, and hollering derogatory remarks. As Venus gathered up the strength to overcome her fear, she jumped into action.

She placed her bags on the ground quietly and walked directly toward them. When she realized the figure on the ground was in fact her mother, she freaked out. One thing led to another, but all Venus remembered was letting off six rounds into the man who was trying to beat her mother to death. As the figure fell to the ground facedown, she grabbed her mother and they both began to run.

Venus's man had given her an ivory handled .22 for Christmas, advising her to use it if ever she came across a problem. It seemed strange at the time, because a man didn't usually give their woman a handgun as a gift. Nevertheless, she had it, so she used it. To her, there was no other way to handle the situation. This was the biggest violation anyone could have ever committed. Fucking with her mother was out of the question. It didn't matter if her mother was an addict. It didn't matter that her mother lied, cheated, stole, and sometimes sold her ass to get the next fix. That was Venus's one and only—the woman who had given her life. Right or wrong, she had to protect her.

After barricading the front door, they had paced around the apartment. Venus had to figure out what to do next. She couldn't believe she had just killed somebody. She could hear her mother mumbling something about "Maybe he's not dead, Vee," but Venus was sure. There were too many voices screaming in her head. She had begun to question her own sanity. Venus had to come up with a story quickly.

She asked her mother to start thinking of something to tell the police just in case they were on to her. However, she wasn't any help. She was too hysterical to think straight. Finally, after several minutes of silence, her mother said to tell them the truth. "The truth shall set you free," is what she said as she dialed 911. To this day, Venus couldn't understand why her mother had done that. In all reality, her own mother had turned her in.

Murder in the second degree, fifteen years, and a whole new way of life is what Venus got for her good deed. Losing the kids was the biggest slap in the face. BCW had taken custody of them, leaving Venus to never see them again.

* * * * *

Venus had drifted back to the night her life had changed. No, she didn't want to talk about it with Damion just yet. Tonight was a new beginning, a chance to live a normal life.

"Hey, baby girl, you alright?" Damion asked, becoming worried for her.

Her blank stare petrified him. He hadn't meant to push her. Maybe he had picked the wrong time to bring any of that shit up.

"Yeah, I'm fine. You took me off guard, that's all. Now can we just have a good time?" Venus said, as she smiled that million-dollar smile, grabbed his hand, and pulled him onto the dance floor.

The evening had turned out to be a huge success, with promises of calling and seeing each other again. Damion walked Venus to Brenda's front door, kissed her softly on the cheek, and thanked her for a great evening.

"Thanks, girl, I had a nice time."

"So did I. I should be the one thanking you."

"Yeah, you're right."

Venus was getting used to his sweet sense of humor, so she giggled.

"Hey, what's so funny?"

"You."

"Oh, really?"

"On a serious note, I really enjoyed myself tonight. Maybe on our next date, I'll share more of myself."

"Venus, you are not the only one who has had it rough. We have all been through some trials and tribulations."

With that being said, Damion turned around and walked down the hall with a big smile on his face. She was the one—that much he knew. The one he could spend the rest of his life with. But first, he had some unfinished business he had to take care of.

Sexy

Chapter 11

Venus closed the door behind her. Quietly, she walked into the living room, removed her three-inch stilettos, and threw her overwhelmed body onto the couch. Gripping one of the many throw pillows Brenda had spread out along the sofa, she cried silently. It had been a long time since she had thought about that night, the night her heart had been torn to pieces.

While imprisoned, Venus had learned to program her mind to never think about it. She also had programmed her heart to never feel the pain of being separated from her child. Forgetting her was something different altogether. She always wondered where she was, what she was doing, and how her life had turned out. Angel was sixteen years old now. Venus wondered if she was happy, what her favorite color was, and what she liked to eat. What books did she like to read? What were her favorite subjects? Did she have a boyfriend? So many questions ran through her mind throughout the years.

She also wondered if Angel's adopted mother knew how hard it had been for her to sign those papers, giving up her parental rights. It was an unselfish act on her part. That's what the social worker told her as she signed her daughter away. The most difficult part was not being able to say goodbye to her. The social worker had thought it would be unhealthy considering the fact that she was about to go to prison for fifteen years, and unhealthy for Angel, too. Venus had watched as the years went by at Bedford, how the inmates suffered after attending visits and holiday get-togethers provided by the Children's Center. She longed to participate in all of those activities. However, the price she would have to pay afterwards was something she could have done without.

Damion had stirred up all those feelings in her—feelings that were long buried inside. He reminded Venus that she could never run away from her past, which was a part of her that could never go away. However, the pain of those memories was unbearable.

Venus curled up in a fetal position and fell asleep with her daughter's little face in mind.

* * * * *

Let the games begin. As soon as Damion arrived home from his date with Venus, he called the Watch Commander at Sing-Sing, and told him that he needed his brother to call home ASAP. There was an emergency with the family and he needed to be informed. After several minutes of trying to convince him that it was not a prank call, the Watch Commander took all the information down so he could forward the message to the officer down on Devon's block. Devon immediately called home.

"What's up, Dey? Is everything alright?"

Devon's hands were unsteady as he held the phone to his ear. He always feared something terrible would happen to one of his family members while he was incarcerated.

"Yeah, why?"

"Don't answer a question with a question, Dey. I thought something really happened."

"Well, it did, and before you go off the deep end, let me tell you that I decided to make that move for you."

"Word!"

"Word, and there's one other thing you need to know."

"What?"

"You better not make me regret it. You do what you got to do and get your ass back up there."

"Yo, bro, that's my word. You will never regret it. I promise you that."

"So is everything set?" Damion asked, while pouring himself a tall glass of cognac.

"Yeah. This is how it's going to go down."

With all the details in mind, Damion ended the call and took a deep breath. He thought about Venus and vowed to make her a part of his life once he returned from his little adventure.

Damion then walked into his bathroom, turned on the lights, and looked into the familiar mirror. However, what he saw looking back was not what he was supposed to see. He grabbed his barber's kit and began his transformation. Part of the plan was to shave, removing all facial hair. Devon had suggested that they remove the hair from their heads and go completely bald, a look Damion wasn't too thrilled about. However, they needed to look exactly alike. What better way than to get rid of their own individuality and become one.

That was the easy part. The actual switch depended on Marcus.

* * * * *

The next morning, Damion rose out of bed from a restless night of staring up at the ceiling. He had not once closed his eyes. Jaz and Toni woke up wrapped in each other's arms, neither aware of what the day would bring. That's how life is. One never expected danger or foul play to come their way until the shit hit the fan.

Devon's cell door began to open. The clicking sound of the gate that separated him from the rest was the sound he had been waiting for. His visit was there.

While he walked down the tier and past the guard, the key turner noticed his makeover.

"Yo, Aviles."

"Yeah, what's up?"

"Good look, man. You think that shit would look good on me?"

"Yeah, why not? Try it."

"Alright, man, maybe I will. You lookin' real slick."

"Have a good one."

"Good looking'."

Devon turned quickly and headed for the exit, thinking, *Damn, that shit was not good.*

The C.O.'s at Sing-Sing noticed everything. Devon was already paranoid, but he couldn't stop now. It was now or never.

Damion looked at his surroundings, as he walked among the other visitors. He had hoped that the visiting room would be crowded, and it was. It was 12:35 p.m., a perfect time. Half of the C.O.'s assigned to this particular post were out to lunch, leaving only two C.O.'s to tend to the many visits all going on at once. There was one at the front desk, who was busy registering the visitors. Then there was one leaning up against a bare wall at the center of the floor. That was the one that Damion needed to keep an eye on.

Although his new look made him *feel* self-conscious, he would have to make sure he didn't *look* self-conscious.

Table 35 was tucked away at the back of the visiting floor. *How convenient,* Damion thought, as he pulled out his seat and sat down. The V.I. began to fill to capacity. Everyone else was so engrossed in their visits that no one noticed him or his brother, who had just stepped through the gate. Devon walked in his direction as though he didn't have a care in the world.

Damion sat completely still, waiting for his brother to approach the table. He couldn't get over the fact that after all these years, they still looked so much alike. It was unbelievable the resemblance.

"Are you ready, Dey?" Devon asked, as Damion sat down on the blue seat designated for visitors. Again, nobody noticed.

"Yeah, but I need to ask you something."

"Go ahead."

"Are you sure you want to do this? Is this the right thing?"

"Listen," Devon said, becoming irritated. "It's too late to be asking me these questions. It's now or never."

"Okay, okay, chill. I just wanted to make sure you know what you're getting us into."

"I know this is not easy for you, but we have to do this."

"Okay, I'm ready," Damion said.

"Alright, just act normal. In a few minutes, shit is about to get crazy in here. Don't panic. Just follow the plan."

Ten minutes later, Damion heard a woman from the far end of the visiting room begin to scream. It was apparent that she was not too happy with the man she had come to see. Cursing and yelling caused everyone to turn their attention in her direction.

"You stupid motherfucker, you think I'm going to allow you to disrespect me after all the shit I've done for you."

The woman jumped up out of her seat and began to beat the shit out of him. Damion looked towards his brother, who was enjoying the show. When Damion looked back in the direction of the couple, he then realized they were the decoys Devon had told him about. That was Marcus at the far end of the room getting the shit beat out of him. It was kind of funny, but there was no time to laugh. He had recognized Marcus from the pictures Devon had sent him earlier that week.

Damion and Devon were now watching the C.O., who stood by the wall and had yet to move. Devon waited a few seconds before he began a countdown. Finally, the C.O. began to move, but not fast enough. The woman continued to yell, becoming louder by the minute, as she watched the C.O. out of the corner of her eye.

"Marcus, this stupid motherfucker ain't moving fast enough. Do something," the woman whispered, then slapped him across the face.

That's when Marcus leaped from his seated position, grabbed the table in front of him, and tossed it, slamming it against a wall. Then he grabbed the Italian actress that stood only 5'3" tall and pulled her closer to him. He told her softly that she was about to play the best role of her life.

Marcus bum rushed her, lifting her by the arms.

"Bitch, are you fuckin' crazy? You do what the fuck I tell you to do. I know you don't think that you're the only bitch that comes up here to hit a nigga off!" Marcus barked, while holding her up eye to eye.

Then and only then did the C.O. rush over.

"Now, Dey," Devon said in a low voice.

The brothers both jumped up and began to remove their clothes. They had sixty seconds to undress and dress again, and then sit down as though nothing had ever happened.

By the time the C.O. reached Marcus, he already had pulled the pin attached to his walkie talkie, alerting the other officers at the facility that there was a problem in the visiting room.

Out of the corner of his eye, Marcus watched the twins as he counted. There was no room for mistakes...56, 57, 58, 59, 60. Then he released the woman, and turned around to find himself face to face with Officer Frost.

"Chill, let me explain."

"There ain't shit to explain. Put your fuckin' hands up over your head and shut the fuck up. Don't say a word."

Naturally, Marcus complied. The twins had safely accomplished the switch, so there was no need for Marcus to get crazy. Lisa Ramano fell to the ground, crying as though her life had come to an end.

"How can you do this to me after everything we've been through? Howwww!!!"

"Ma'am, are you alright?" C.O. Frost asked, while bending down to lift the young woman from the ground.

"No, you fuckin' asshole. Do I look alright?" Lisa yelled into the palms of her hands.

"Ma'am, I'm going to have to ask you to please leave this visiting floor. Your visit has been terminated."

Officer Frost had never witnessed such cruelty. The men he guarded on a day-to-day basis were much more grateful to get visits. He didn't know Marcus, and after this display, he didn't want to know him. He had three years left until retirement, and he refused to leave with any damage done to his persona. He wasn't about to get physically involved. He felt that he was too old for this bullshit. He would leave the rough stuff for the younger generation of C.O.'s coming in.

Marcus stood on the sidelines as Officer Frost escorted Lisa to the front desk. By the time he returned, Marcus was handcuffed. He had just bought himself a one-way ticket to SHU, a special housing unit designed for problem inmates.

Meanwhile, Devon and Damion sat speechless. It soon became obvious to them that they were in the clear. The clock on the wall read 2:55 p.m., and visits were over at three o'clock.

"I'll be back, Dey. I promise."

"I know you will."

"Visitors, can I please have your attention? Visiting hours are now over," the front desk C.O. announced into the microphone.

Before Devon was about to walk off into his war, Damion called after him, telling him something he hadn't told him in a long time.

"I love you, Bro. Please take care of yourself out there."

Devon turned his head slightly, as tears formed at the corners of his eyes. "I know, Dey, I know. I love you, too, twin."

"Dee, before you leave, promise me you're going to stop by to see Vee. She is special to me."

"I got you. You just take care of yourself in here. If you need anything, look for Marcus."

"Alright."

As the brothers embraced, a rush of electricity ran through their bodies. The connection between them could never be denied.

"Ladies and gentlemen, this is your last call," the officer announced, while walking through the room.

"I have to go. How do I look?"

"You look like me. Now go before I change my mind."

"Alright, I'm out. Be easy."

Devon walked off feeling that for sure he was doing the right thing. He mixed in with the crowd, passed the first set of guards, and walked directly towards the front gate. Once he crossed the threshold, the beast was released to freedom. The beast was suddenly aware and alert.

His first stop would be his mother's place. Devon had to give Jaz the heads-up in case anything went wrong. Someone would have to get Damion out of prison if he got hurt and couldn't get back on time—or worse, if he was killed

Chapter 12

The evening that Supreme got the phone call letting him know that Devon had passed on, he had Twista drive him around the hood. They rode around for several hours in silence, contemplating what to do next, and made the Washington Projects their final destination. Supreme hoped to run into one of Devon's family members. If, in fact, Devon was dead, the people in the projects would be in an uproar since Devon was very much liked by everyone. There would be a lot of excitement and confusion throughout the "D." There would be word of his death among the neighbors.

Supreme sat in the backseat of his brand-new Cadillac Escalade. He observed his surroundings, glanced down Third Avenue, then stepped out of the truck. It was time to make his rounds. He strapped two .45 Magnums to his waistband, zipped his leather bomber closed, and then headed towards the entrance. His attitude was that of a true kingpin— confident, strong, and fearless.

With Twista close behind him, he saw a group of youngens sitting around on a broken down wooden bench. They happened to be in front of 1955, the building where Devon's mother still resided. It soon became obvious that word had not circulated the way Supreme had hoped.

Sexy

Outside of the small group, the project buildings were dead. There wasn't a soul in sight, except for a few crack heads moving quickly back and forth searching for their next hit.

"What's up, little fellows? What y'all doing?"

"Who wants to know?" asked a funny looking kid with crooked teeth.

"Yo, chill, Crook," said one of the others. "That's Supreme."

"Who the fuck is Supreme?"

"Watch your mouth, little guy. Didn't your people teach you any manners?" Supreme smirked. *Too bad this nigga is too young. I would definitely put him on my team,* Supreme thought to himself, as he looked down on him.

"Don't be talkin' about my people, you sucker-ass nigga." Crook jumped up off the bench.

"Yo, you got a lot of heart for a brother who is still wet behind the ears."

The projects came to life by the roar of Supreme's laugh. He found Crook's spunk amusing, so he chose to allow Crook to get his thug on.

"Chill, little man. I didn't mean no harm."

"So why you all up in this place asking questions? Don't you see you're invading a nigga's space?"

Supreme held his composure. The tension was getting thick. The disrespect was beginning to penetrate.

"How old are you, little man?"

"Why?"

"'Cause you're too young to be out here trying to gang bang."

"I ain't young. Fifteen is old enough. I've been out here a long time. What's your story?" Crook asked, while stepping in closer.

"Yo, check this out. Let me holler at you for a second."

They both moved over to the side with caution. Crook hesitated, half-stepping.

"Come on, little man; let me talk to you for a minute."

Little Man is what Supreme chose to call him because he really didn't want to get to know the boy's name. All Supreme wanted was some information.

"Yeah, what's up?"

"First of all, be easy. Ain't no need to be so hostile. All I want is to ask you a few questions."

"What? I ain't got time for the games."

Supreme let that response ride, too.

"Do you know Jaz and Toni?"

"Who? The two dykes? Yeah, I know them. Why?"

"They are friends of mine, and I heard that one of their sons was knocked off in the P-Nile."

"I don't know. I seen them earlier today, and everything was everything."

"Did they look upset or anything?"

"Nah, man. They look alright to me."

"Did you hear anything at all about Devon's death?"

"Devon? Nah, man, but if that's true, that's twisted. That was a good nigga."

"Yeah, I know. That's why I'm here. I wanted to give his fam my condolences."

"You want me to go and find out?"

"Nah, I don't want to upset them if it ain't true. I'm just going to fall back and see what the streets are talking about."

Supreme reached into his pocket, pulled out a wad of hundred dollar bills, and peeled off a few bills. He handed them over to Crook.

"Alright, little man, thanks. Good looking out. Go buy yourself something other than some weed. That shit slows you down."

"Thanks." Crook grabbed the money, shoved it into his jeans pocket, and then walked back over to where his boys were.

Twista crept up beside Supreme. "So what's good?"

"Twista, something ain't right."

"I know, boss. Maybe it's all bullshit."

"Yeah, I was thinking the same thing. Let's get the fuck out of here."

They quickly exited the park area, jumped into the truck, and sped off.

Supreme needed to get to the bottom of things. If Toy lied to him, he was a dead man.

* * * * *

Missing Supreme by seconds, Devon had reached his mother's apartment building unnoticed. Nothing had really changed around the neighborhood since his incarceration. The building where he had grown up still had graffiti on the walls. The smell of urine still lingered in the air, becoming a natural scent—something to be expected in the projects. Like always, the elevators were broken, so Devon had to take the stairs to his mother's apartment. Things had not changed around the hood, but he knew that behind his mother's door, things were about to change drastically. He thought about how his mother was going to react, as he climbed the steps two at a time.

He had thought about how the two of them switching places was going to affect the family. His reasons had all been good at that moment. However, now he wasn't so sure. Devon reached for the steel knocker and banged on the door twice, letting Jaz know that it was someone known to the family. He waited.

He could hear Marvin Gaye's "Let's Get It On" in the background. Toni was home, that much was for sure. She was the one to sit around and listen to oldies but goodies. Jaz was more into the modern R&B. The twins had grown up on that type of music. It took him back to when he was a little boy. That was a time when there weren't any complications in his life.

"Who is it?"

Devon froze. He had hoped that his mother wasn't home. Not sure how he would break the news to her, he would rather deal with Toni first.

"Who is it?" Jaz hollered once again, hoping that whoever it was had gone away. She wasn't in the mood for company.

Devon took a deep breath. "It's me, Mom. Open the door."

Jaz walked quickly towards the door and looked through the peephole. She wanted to be sure it was her baby and not some crazy motherfucker trying to catch a sting. The projects had turned into a war zone. It just wasn't safe anymore. It wasn't at all like when she first moved in. The intercom system was always being vandalized, leaving the building open for unwanted company.

Jaz opened the door and held her arms wide. She needed to be filled with the love only her sons knew how to give.

"Hi, baby, come on in. Give Mami a big kiss."

Devon looked at his mother from head to toe. She was still gorgeous after all these years. Her long black hair was now cut in layers, forming a feathered look around her oval-shaped face. Her eyes were still bright, but if you looked deeply, you could see the hint of sadness that only added to her sex appeal. Yeah, she was indeed one beautiful woman.

Devon was extremely proud of his mother. She always gave her all. When it came to the ones she loved, there were no limits. Now embraced by her loving arms, Devon had to tell her the truth—or did he?

Gently pulling her in closer, Devon whispered, "What's up, Mom? How you doing?"

"I'm good, baby. What's wrong?"

She could feel his body tense up. Jaz tried to pull away. Something wasn't right.

"Baby, what's wrong?"

"Shhhh, Mom. I just need to hold you."

Devon's eyes became misty. He never realized how much he missed her. When Jaz was finally able to escape his grip, she stepped back and looked into her son's eyes. She didn't need much searching to know that it was not Damion who had stepped across her threshold. It was Devon. Jaz still leaned in to get a better look. There was no mistaking the two.

"Oh, my God," were the last words Jaz said before she fainted, falling to the ground.

When she came to, she found herself lying on top of her sectional leather sofa. How she had gotten there was beyond her. She looked around in desperation, and terror struck immediately as she remembered what had transpired. Devon was sitting at the far end of the sofa, and Toni—well, she was trying to place a cold washcloth on Jaz's forehead.

"Jaz, wake up, baby. I know you ain't buggin' 'cause our baby's home."

Toni couldn't stop smiling. She hadn't found it strange at all that Damion and Devon had come up with such an outrageous plan. Toni was used to them playing the old switcheroo game. While Jaz was out, Devon had been able to tell Toni what he had done, and she wasn't surprised.

"Stop calling me a baby, Papa!" Devon said.

Devon had always referred to Toni as Papa. Being that Toni portrayed the male figure in her relationship with Jaz, Papa was the name the boys had decided to use. Devon had to give props where props were due. Toni had definitely earned that title. Not only did Toni love and respect his mother, Toni loved him and Damion as though they were her own sons.

"Not right now, Dee. I'm trying to get your mother right."

"Yeah, alright. This is how you do that. Yo, Mom, get up. I need to talk to you," Devon screamed.

Jaz began to stir and moan from the headache. She touched the side of her head to find a knot.

"I must have hit that floor pretty hard, huh?"

Now with Devon in full view, she jumped off the sofa, grabbed Devon by the head—stroking, touching, kissing every inch of him. She couldn't believe it.

"Oh, my God, my baby is home. Thank you, Jesus."

"Mom, chill. Wait a minute."

Devon stood up. He didn't want his mother to get the wrong idea. He didn't have a chance to say a word before she began asking a whole bunch of questions.

"Why didn't Damion tell me you had won your appeal? Remind me to kick his ass once he gets here."

"Mom."

"Yeah, baby?"

This was the hardest thing he ever had to do. Devon sighed, walked over to the window and said, "Mom, I didn't win my appeal."

"What do you mean, baby? So how did you get out of jail?"

"I escaped."

"Escaped? Please, boy."

"I'm serious, Mom."

"How the fuck did you manage that? Stop playin' with me," Jaz said, while walking over to stand beside him.

She placed her hand on his shoulder and turned him to face her. There directly in front of her was the son she had lost to the system. Jaz had never given up hope of having him in the free world again, though, but to escape was crazy.

"Mom, I'm not playing. Please sit down and let me explain."

Devon walked her across the room, sat her down, and then began to tell her the details. Jaz was very much aware that her sons had a lot of heart, but she couldn't believe they had come up with a scheme so dangerous.

"What time is it?"

"Why?"

Sexy

"Don't be asking me any fuckin' questions." Jaz was livid. "Why the fuck do you think? I need to go see my son."

"It's too late, Mom. Visiting hours is over."

Jaz had to know for sure that she wasn't having a fucking nightmare. First thing in the morning she would be heading to Sing-Sing.

Chapter 13

Damion walked the unfamiliar corridor to the housing unit where Devon was housed. He followed the yellow line painted on the wall, which directed him and the other inmates to the different areas of the facility. It soon became obvious to him that this would be the easiest way to get around. Walking towards his new home, he realized he was mentally exhausted. It had been a long day, and the privacy of his brother's cell was just what he needed to come to grips with prison life.

Damion had asked his brother questions during their visits, but it just wasn't the same as actually living it. Now he would know what his brother dealt with on a daily basis.

As he reached the block, he heard clicking sounds coming from inside. Damion came to a complete halt, wondering what the sound could be. Then he realized what it was. It didn't take a genius to figure it out. It was the sound of the steel gates opening and allowing inmates' entry. Once the gates opened wide enough for him to pass through, he did. Once in, the transformation began to take place. He had to start acting and speaking like Devon. Damion's formal lingo was not going to make do.

Passing several doors with name tags on them, he immediately noticed there wasn't a whole lot of movement permitted throughout the jail. Access to counselors, nurses, and the Law Library were just beyond his reach. He couldn't begin to imagine how his brother had made it through the last four years. He wouldn't wish this on anyone.

He could remember reading an article in the Village Voice regarding prison suicide. There was one paragraph that always stuck in his mind: The suicide rate behind the walls was much higher now by 90%. Inmates chose death before time.

Why, Damion asked himself, but then answered his own question—because they couldn't cope with the solitude.

Six more days of this, he thought, as he finally walked into the cell block.

"Hey, Aviles. How was your visit?"

"It was alright, Officer."

"Officer? Damn, nigger, I thought we were beyond that."

Damion had no idea that Devon had made friends among the administration. As far as he was concerned, that was a no, no.

"What, you having an out-of-body experience?" the officer questioned.

"Nah, man," Damion said, looking lost.

It would have helped if Devon would have told him that he had some type of connection with the officer who stood before him. Damion made a mental note to ask Devon about it, as well as several other things for that matter.

"Stop playin' with me, Dee," Officer Higgins warned, as he placed his arm around Damion's shoulder.

Damion tried to act as normal as possible. It didn't seem to be working, though. Damion had no idea how Devon was perceived on the inside, so he tried a different approach.

"I'm not playin'. You know you my man. My visit went good. You know a nigga gets ill after a V.I. Don't be taking shit personal."

"Yeah, I know. Be easy, man. Your appeal is going to go through. I got a good feeling about that, dawg."

Officer Higgins removed his hand from Damion's shoulder, and then extended it towards him. They gave each other a pawn before he moved on.

"Shift is changing. See your ass tomorrow. Hold your head."

"Good looking."

Damion moved on as though the closeness between prisoner and officer was a normal thing.

"Right, man. I already popped your cell."

Damion nodded his head, then commenced to walk away. He hoped no one else would stop him.

"Yo, Aviles."

Oh shit, what now? Damion turned his head slowly, looking over his shoulder.

"Yeah?"

"Did you pick up your package?"

Damion had completely forgotten that he had fixed himself a care package with all the things he would need to make his stay bearable.

"Nah, man, I forgot."

"Well, go get it before the count. Damn, nigga, that must have been some V.I. you was on. You're acting mighty strange. You sure you alright?"

"Yeah, I'm good. Tired, I guess."

"Yo, you talkin' mad funny, too. You better watch yourself. Niggas in here are goin' to start thinking you getting soft."

Damion hadn't noticed that his speech had changed again. It was a dead giveaway. He had to polish up his act. Like many, he had to maintain an image.

With that, Damion exited the cell block and headed back in the direction from which he came. Still following the color codes on the wall, he found the package room. Once inside Devon's cell, he tossed everything onto the iron frame that was supposed to be a bed. "Sad" was what he said as he sat down.

He looked at all the pictures that were placed neatly on the wall. There were pictures of Devon and him at home, notes, magazine clippings. As he looked at the pictures of half naked women touching their breast while playin' in their kittys, thoughts of Venus flashed before him.

Devon stood up and walked over to the steel desk that was bolted to the floor by screws the size of golf balls. The administration was not playing when it came to safety. But how much damage can someone make with a desk. He noticed a pile of letters written to Devon by their mother. Damion reached out to touch them, then decided midway not to. They were private correspondence between mother and son. He didn't want to violate his brother's space. He had enough shit in his brown paper bags to keep him busy for the next few days.

Count time came and went, and another day had begun. Cell doors popped open. Men went on with their day, definitely part of a routine. Nothing personal. From the second tier, Damion observed the other men as they hung out in the rec area. Some gathered their belongings to shit, shower, and shave. Some watched sports attentively, their eyes never leaving the 19-inch color TV provided by the New York State Department of Corrections. He even watched how the homo thugs exchanged small love gestures between themselves and their extremely feminine he/she's. The smell of home-cooked meals lingered throughout, awakening his curiosity.

Walking towards the steps that would bring him onto the main floor, Damion began to feel uncomfortable. Hesitant to confront this lifestyle head-on, Damion slowed down. He backed up a little. His palms became sweaty; his forehead was dripping with perspiration. This was not his idea of a good time.

Damion's head was pounding; his brother's voice was not helping either. He could hear Devon telling him that he could do this. *No one knows me better than you. You could play the part. So, play it.* It was as though Devon was standing right beside him.

Damion had to get a hold of himself. If he fucked this up, his brother could get life without parole, or worse the death penalty. He would also go down. The charges against him would be endless. Impersonation would be at the top of the list, and if there wasn't a penal code on that, the D.A. would make some shit up to charge him with.

It never dawned on Damion to ask Devon about his daily routine. Did he play cards? Did he watch the Sports Channel? And if he did, at about what time did these events take place? Or did he conduct his life in the P-Nile the way he did on the street?

Damion was afraid of making any wrong moves. Something out of the ordinary would give him away. Something unexpected would definitely give him away. However, he couldn't hide out in the cell. That would surely bring attention his way. Maybe he would take a shower, relax a little, and then interact with the other convicts. Or maybe he would call home and just ask him. While in the middle of his thoughts, Damion heard one of the C.O.'s calling his name.

"Yeah, what's up?" Damion yelled, as he took the steps two at a time.

"Today is your lucky day. You have another visit."

Damion was now familiar with the route to the visiting room, so he was there in no time.

Jaz had to hold her composure as she watched her bald-headed son walk in her direction. She smiled at her son, but had tears in her eyes.

"Why, baby?"

"Mom, what are you doing here?"

"I'm the one asking the questions, Dey!" Jaz's tone went up a notch."

"Shhh, Mom. Someone may hear you."

"All I want to know is why you would give up your life like this?"

"You're asking me why? Aren't you the one who always told us that no matter what we had to stick together? Aren't you the one who instilled the importance of brotherhood?"

"Yes, but—"

"Mom, there are no buts. Devon has to clear his name. I owe him my life. He gave up his life for me. It's only right that I do the same for him."

Jaz looked at her son. What was she thinking about when she ran out of her apartment, jumped into a cab, and boarded the Metro-North on 125th Street first thing this morning? She knew in her heart that no matter what the circumstances her sons would live and die for each other. They would trust and believe that the other would do what was right. Suddenly, she couldn't help but to feel pride for them both.

"Are you okay?"

"Yes, I'm fine. Don't worry about me. I'll manage. The one you need to worry about is Devon. So, please, go home and handle your business."

"What do you mean handle my business? What am I supposed to do?"

"I want you to be the old Jaz, the do-or-die Jaz; the right, wrong, or indifferent Jaz."

"Is that what you really want from me—to go back into my old ways?"

"Mom, you really don't have a choice. Devon needs all the help he can get."

"Be careful what you ask for, baby. You just may get it."

"That's what I'm counting on," Damion asserted, as he touched his mother's soft face.

Being a loving mother to her sons was all she wanted to do. However, the son's request to protect, kill, or be killed was a whole different story. Hurt and desperation took over. Jaz left the V.I. and went straight to the locker that held her phone. She pressed her speed dial.

"Call in the crew, Tee."

"What! What happened, Jaz?"

"I'll explain when I get there. Tell the Geechies to meet me at the old spot."

"Why, Jaz? What the fuck is going on?"

"Tee!"

"Yeah?"

"Just do it. Now!"

Jaz ended the call and walked out of Sing-Sing with one mission on her mind—to protect Devon. She had vowed to protect her sons from the minute they came into this world. She would give her life for them both. So, if that's what she needed to do, then so be it.

Sexy

Chapter 14

Devon paced around the apartment like a mad man. He wasn't expecting his mother to react the way that she did. She was from the old school. Becoming emotional wasn't part of her character. He honestly believed she would have taken the news of their switch lightly. He needed his mother to be levelheaded.

As he continued to pace back and forth, he overheard Toni in the bedroom talking to someone on the phone. Devon didn't want to disrespect Toni by ear hustling, but what choice did he have?

"What do you mean she's called in the crew?"

Devon listened from the doorway. He had no idea who was on the other end of the phone line. All he knew was that it didn't sound good.

"Alright, alright, I hear you. What do you want me to do? You know Jaz; once she sets her mind on something it's a done deal. You just keep me informed, okay? Oh yeah, and another thing, you guys better take care of my lady."

Still listening, Devon took a deep breath. He had heard enough.

Toni hung the phone up and walked over to her bedroom entrance.

"Dee, come on in. I know you overheard my conversation. From the sound of things, your mom has called in the crew."

"What's happening, Toni?"

"Your mom has called a meeting with the Geechies and Chase. I don't know what happened on that visit, but I do know one thing, your mom is not taking this shit lightly."

"I was thinking the same thing, Tee. It sounds like shit is getting ready to get crunked up."

"Listen, Dee, do you remember all those stories you heard about your mom and Aunt Trouble?"

"Yeah."

"Well, they are all true. Your mom is no joke, kid. You're getting ready to meet the ultimate bitch."

Devon smiled at Toni's choice of words. He had always wondered what his mother was like back in the day. Now he was about to find out.

* * * * *

Jaz parked her truck on Fifth Avenue, away from the park entrance. Looking up the side of the street and back again, she turned off the ignition and reached for her .38 special. Before she reached her final destination, Jaz first made a quick stop at Julio's old grocery store.

Right after her boys were born, Jaz had gotten rid of all her guns and ammunition, all except for the .38 special she now held in her hand. Jaz knew that one day she would be in need of it again. This is why she had decided to hide it at the Geechie's stash house, which was located in the basement of Julio's grocery store. What better place than where the Geechies held the rest of their treasures.

She tucked the gun into her waistband, and then zipped up her leather Gucci jacket. As she entered the park, flashbacks of her days in the streets crossed her mind.

She found that the meeting bench was still in its place, along with all of the crew members—Cookie, Lizzy, Tima, Evelyn, and, of course, Trouble. Chase was somewhere in the cut. His presence was sensed.

Jaz didn't greet anyone with formality. She went straight to the core of things by telling them that her boys were in trouble and that she needed their help. The target: Supreme. The plan: Conquer and destroy.

* * * * *

Devon had so much to do. First, he had to get in touch with Venus. Damion had made him promise to contact her, so he would call to make some excuse as to why he couldn't see her today and then go on about his business.

"Hello. Can I speak to Venus?"

"What's up, Dey," Brenda sang into the phone.

"What's up, baby girl? I just called to check in with you."

"Dey, you must be buggin'. This ain't Venus. This is Brenda. What, you don't recognize your woman's voice?"

"Oh shit, my bad. What's up? Is Venus there?"

Damn, Damion never mentioned this chick Brenda. He almost fucked up.

"Yeah, hold on. Vee, it's your knight in shining armor, girl. Pick up the other line."

Venus ran across the wooden floor in her bare feet, dove across the bed like an Olympic diver, and grabbed the phone that sat on the nightstand.

She must be really feeling this nigga, Brenda thought, as she watched her friend touch her chest and take a deep breath before she spoke.

"Hello."

"Venus, is that you?"

"Yeah."

Like an actor, he picked up right on cue. "What's up? What you doing?"

"Nothing much. Just chillin'. I was getting ready to lay my head down."

"Lay your head down? It's ten o'clock in the morning."

"Yeah, I know, but I went to Barnes & Noble's last night and picked up this new book entitled *Chained*. I stayed up all night reading. So I was about to just fall back and rest a little. Why? Do you have other plans for me tonight?"

Venus was mischievous. She didn't want to come off as a fast ass, but she was really feeling Damion. After their first date, all she thought about was riding his pony. It had been a long time since she had any type of desire for a man.

"Baby, why don't you come pick me up?"

Devon was not prepared for that. He had much more important matters to attend to. Being rude was not in his brother's nature, so he had to get out of this as smoothly as possible.

"I have plans for today, Vee, but maybe tomorrow."

"What do you mean you have plans, Dey?"

"Yeah, it's like I said, I have plans."

Devon's voice was cold. He felt the chill himself, but it was too late. What was said was already said.

"You know what? I don't know what your problem is, and honestly I don't give a fuck. Why did you even bother to call if you were going to play yourself? You're not the man I thought you were. Do me a favor and lose this number."

Venus slammed the phone in his ear.

Devon fucked up and he knew it. He could have kicked his own ass, which he would have much rather done now than what his brother would do later. He had to remember that he was playing out his brother's life, not his. So, he redialed the number. He had to find a way to make this shit up to her. Damion would be tight if he got word that he disrespected his girl. *Damn!*

"What the fuck do you want, Dey?" Venus answered, after the third ring. "I told you not to call me anymore."

"Chill, Vee. I'm sorry, girl. I've been under a lot of pressure."

"Pressure? You want to talk about pressure? I went on three job interviews today, and guess what? I was rejected before I even walked through the fuckin' door because of my criminal history. And you want to talk to me about pressure?"

Criminal history! What the fuck did Damion get himself into? His brother never dated anyone who had done time or lived outside the law. Damion had always gone outside the hood to meet broads. *There must be something special about this one. This is going to be interesting.*

"Venus, listen. I'ma see you tonight for a few minutes, but remember, I have something I need to take care of, alright?"

"Okay, baby. I'll meet you in front of the building. What time? Does nine o'clock sound good?"

Devon had no idea where the front of her building was. He had forgotten to get all of the details. Damion and Devon were so focused on the switch that the little things that could blow their cover had slipped their minds.

"Where you at?"

"What you mean, where I'm at? Dey, you are acting strange. What's wrong with you?"

"Nothing, just tell me where you're staying."

"On 135th Street at Lenox. What, you don't remember where you dropped me off?"

"Nah, man. Just meet me on the corner and wear something red."

"Why?"

"'Cause it's my favorite color, and stop asking me so many questions. Just wear it."

Again, Venus told him he was acting strange. But it was all good. She would be there.

"Okay, baby, I'll see you tonight."

Devon had never seen her before, not even in pictures. With the red on, it would be much easier to spot her.

Damion had left the keys to his Lexus SUV right where he said he would. The cell phone and funds he requested were all in place, as well.

Before he headed out the door, Devon left Toni instructions regarding his mother. Just twenty-four hours on the street and his mother was on the prowl calling in the troops. And as if he didn't have enough problems, he had to go and stroke some chick that didn't belong to him. Devon could do without all of the drama women brought to the table. All he wanted was to clear his mind so he could go on with his life.

On his way to Harlem, he thought about Supreme. Tonight he would meet Toy, who by some strange reason had been released first thing that morning. Toy was the pawn Devon would use to capture Supreme's trifling ass.

* * * * *

Venus and Brenda had begun a ritual. On Friday nights, right before Brenda closed down the shop, she walked around selecting different outfits that they would wear over the course of the weekend. With tags still in place and garments right out of the dry cleaners, no one noticed the difference. Without a second thought, Brenda would place them back on the rack Monday morning. It just so happened, Gucci had just come out with a new line of full-piece, tight-fitting leather suits, and Brenda had one hanging on her bedroom door in the color was red.

"If this shit doesn't knock him off his feet, nothing will," Venus said to Brenda, as she began to dress.

Chapter 15

Toy admired the black Hummer with dark tinted windows.

"Damn that's nice!"

"Yeah, whoever is riding home in that is one lucky motherfucka," the guard who was escorting him towards freedom said, as they walked side by side. "Is that you?" the guard asked, continuing on in his quest for information, which was something all guards did, even up to the very end of a nigga's bid.

"Nah, I ain't that lucky motherfucka," Toy said, while tossing his black duffle bag over his shoulder. "But who knows? I could be riding in one of those real soon," Toy added, throwing that in for good measure.

The Iron Gate clicked open, and Toy eased through. Finally, he was on the side that he wanted to be on. Once standing in the main parking lot of Sing-Sing, he again glanced toward the Hummer, wondering who was inside. Without so much as a second thought, he moved on.

He knew the route to New York City all too well. It was one traveled by him many times before. The only difference was that this time he wasn't coming back in this direction. Toy had moved on from slinging crack cocaine on the corner—mentally at least. Thanks to Supreme's strong desire to be rid of Devon, Toy met the one nigga that would fatten his pockets.

Toy looked back at the prison that once held his body. However, one thing he knew for sure, it never held his soul. That belonged to him no matter where he was. Taking the final turn, he walked down the path that led to the bus stop.
Silently, the Hummer came to life and began moving forward. Slowly, the driver guided the vehicle closely behind Toy.

Toy tensed up. When once he wasn't sure, he now was. Whoever was in the truck was there to see him. The Hummer pulled up alongside of him as he tried to quicken his step. Then it stopped. Toy stopped, too. The passenger side window began to roll down. Midway, Toy got a better look at the uninvited guest.

So much had gone down behind the walls that sometimes niggas never made it home on their release date. He hoped this was not one of those times. Toy didn't want to be a statistic. He didn't want to be the nigga on the front page of tomorrow's *Daily News*.

Flashes of how the headline would read passed across his mind: *Recently released inmate found murdered in abandoned alleyway with several gunshot wounds to the head.* Nah, he didn't want to go out like that. The thought alone brought chills to his spine.

Not recognizing the man who stared out of the lowered glass, Toy stood there a few seconds frozen in fear. Maybe it was a case of mistaken identity. However, the eye contact between them was fierce.

"Yo, what's good, nigga? Supreme wants to see you."

Toy's mind began to race. This was not supposed to go down like this.

"Shit," Toy mumbled under his breath.

He had made his plans with Devon. What the fuck was he going to do now? Supreme had no idea that he didn't go through with the hit. Or did he? Toy hadn't noticed anything in Supreme's voice when they had spoken.

He had to find the nerve to play his position, and that he would. What choice did he have?

The bugged out thing was that he couldn't get in touch with Devon's twin to inform him that there had been a change of plans.

"So where's he at?"

"Get in. I'ma take you to him."

"What are you waiting for? An invitation?" another voice said from inside the truck as the backdoor opened.

Toy swung his bag onto the backseat and jumped in. The truck sped away from the prison grounds before he was able to shut the door behind him.

Supreme was waiting patiently by the FDR Drive. He sat by the pier overlooking the bridge that led to Wards Island. On that same bridge, Michael Jackson and Diana Ross had filmed the movie *The Wiz*. Supreme smiled at the thought.

Lighting the purple haze he held in his hand, he breathed in deeply. Depending on his vibe, he would have to dispose of him quickly, execution style. He wouldn't have it any other way. Supreme had a gut feeling that something had gone wrong with the order issued. He had selected this lowlife, riffraff, wannabe gangster motherfucka because he came cheap. Niggas in the P-Nile didn't need much money to live on. Fifty thousand dollars would go a long way for a petty-ass, low-level drug pusher. Toy's lack of dignity let him settle for anything.

Finally, the Hummer climbed onto the ramp. Taking his last deep drag from the blunt, Supreme stood with his back to the river.

Twista opened the backdoor, pulling Toy out by his arm. Toy struggled to free himself from Twista's grip, but couldn't. Twista had a strong hold on him. Supreme found that shit funny, and with each step that Toy took towards him, he laughed.

Sexy

He felt the evilness that lurked within. Anyone who dealt with him knew he was one evil motherfucka when pushed to that point. Supreme had programmed his mind to never feel, especially when it came to business.

He walked among the living dead—just like the crack heads he sold his poison to. It was easier not to feel. That way, emotions didn't get in the way of what he needed to do. The streets had taught him lessons on humanity. Kindness or mercy was weak points for a hustler. The streets had taught him about the dark side. Supreme had become reckless in his dealings. Most of all, he had become secretive, not letting his left hand know what his right hand was doing. Getting rid of damaged goods had become second nature to him. Supreme was going to give Toy the benefit of the doubt, though, but if he didn't come through on some real shit, then he would be one less nigga to worry about.

Supreme tried to hold his composure as Toy got closer. He could sense the fear and terror that hid behind Toy's eyes. Yet, Toy held his ground.

"Supreme, what's up, man? Tell your man to be easy."

"Stop crying, bitch!" Supreme tossed the rest of the blunt into the river, then stepped forward to meet Toy eye to eye.

The pressure from Twista's grip was beginning to hurt. His eyes zeroed in on Supreme, while asking him again to tell his boy to be easy.

Toy's biggest mistake at this point was to show any signs of weakness. His life depended on what he was going to say next. Additionally, he wasn't about to give Supreme the satisfaction of seeing him sweat—not in this lifetime anyway.

"Welcome home, nigga," Supreme greeted.

"Thanks, dawg."

"The reason my boy brought you out here is because I need to know something, so tell me."

"Tell you what, Sup? I told you everything I needed to when we spoke last," Toy said, as he wiped the sweat forming on his hands. "Oh shit," he said, looking deeper into Supreme's eyes. "You want details?"

Supreme nodded his head up and down.

"Oh, so this is what all of this is about? When, where, how, and you already know the reason why. It was your idea, right?"

Supreme nodded his head yes again.

"Well, I don't think none of that shit matters. When, where, and how is irrelevant."

"Those little details may be irrelevant to you, smart-ass, but not to me," Supreme continued. "It's funny how I haven't heard nothing on the streets about Devon's death. The family is acting normal as hell. You see, Toy, I know Dee and his people. And if they knew that Dee was murdered in the P-Nile, his people would lose their minds, especially his mom."

"Well, I don't know what to tell you, Sup. All I do know is that I executed the hit."

"You sure about that?"

"Yeah, I'm sure. I personally took care of it myself."

"Alright, dawg. You better be straight up with me, because if you ain't, be ready to die."

Supreme stated his last words, then walked past Toy and told Twista to get into the truck.

Just like that they were gone—for now. Toy bent over to relieve the stomach cramp that had formed. Once the cramp subsided, he lifted his bag that Twista had tossed out of the truck, and then walked away from the pier.

* * * * *

Venus was looking anxiously out the window, when she saw Damion's Lexus SUV pull up to the curb. She still couldn't figure out what she had done so well in her life to have received such a blessing. Not only did she find a man with a J.O.B., but she had found a man who had style and grace.

Venus was not trying to get herself caught up with no street niggas like her daughter's father. Street thugs were not on today's menu. Those days were long gone. The only thing she ever thought about was her baby brother Marcus, whom she would touch base with once she got on her feet. Through some help from her P.O., she had discovered that Marcus was doing time at Sing-Sing.

The time would come when Venus would make contact, but not yet. She was not about to go up there empty-handed. She wanted to reassure her brother that life didn't have to be so complicated. But first, she had to show him through her own success.

Venus grabbed her purse, then dashed through the apartment and out the front door. Taking the steps down two at a time, she found herself on the sidewalk in no time. Venus then turned on her heels and strolled down the street with her bootylious attitude—confident that she looked good in her red, skin-tight, leather two-piece cat suit and 3-inch red stilettos. She wore her hair pulled up into a messy bun held by two red Chinese chopsticks. Soft curls fell to the sides, giving her an exotic 'come-fuck-me' look.

Venus tried to ignore all of the compliments, whistles, and sly remarks coming from the men who hung around doing nothing all day. If it weren't for that one fact, she probably would have responded with a smile. They were not her cup of tea. Damion was the man she wanted, and that man was the one she was out to get.

Walking straight towards the corner with her head held high, suddenly coming into his view, Venus stopped dead in her tracks and posed. Before he was able to get out of the truck, Venus wanted him to get the full effect.

Devon's eyes must have been deceiving him. *The chick in the red suit couldn't possibly be Venus,* he thought, as he noticed his dick getting rock hard. He envisioned them fucking, sweating, butt-ass naked and spread across a king-size bed—doing the damn thing. He envisioned her stroking his dick with one hand while inserting it into her warm mouth with the other.

From the sound of her voice, he thought he was going to meet the stuck-up type. The type of bitch that thought she was too good. To his surprise, he was wrong. This chick was straight-up hood. Devon could tell by the way she stood there waiting on him. He liked her already.

Devon stroked his dick, tucking it between his legs so it would go down before he emerged onto the sidewalk. As soon as he had control of his organ, he opened the door and jumped out. Pulling his pants softly away from his crotch, he walked over to Venus. Standing directly in front of her, he glanced at her full figure. Devon couldn't help but to wonder what it would be like to knock her boots, break her back, and make her scream his name. The reality was, though, she wouldn't be screaming his name as he pounded his manhood into her wet pussy. She would be screaming out his brother's name.

"What a shame," he spoke softly, with a sly smirk on his face.

"What a shame? And why are you looking at me like that, baby?" Venus asked with confusion in her tone.

Did he like the outfit or didn't he? She wanted to make his jaw drop, to get a 'you-look-good' response. Instead, she received a 'you-look-like-a-hoochie' look.

"Don't you like my outfit? If not, I'll go up and change real quick. I thought it was a little too much, being that it's so early and all. This is more like a 'go-out-all-night and dance-your-ass-off' type of outfit."

Venus was babbling on. She didn't know what the fuck to say, but she most definitely didn't want to turn Damion off.

"Nah, baby, your ass looks good, and I mean that shit literally."

"Oh yeah! Well, thank you. That's exactly what I wanted to hear."

She moved in closer to kiss him on the lips softly.

"You look good, too, baby, but what's up with your gear? I know you don't go to work dressed like that. Did you play hooky without me?" Venus asked with a devilish tone.

Devon was enjoying himself.

"And what about your hair? What, are you tryin' to get ghetto fabulous on me?"

Thinking fast, Devon came back with, "I thought being baldheaded, wearing Ecko jeans, and a white T-shirt would ease our relationship a little. Look, I even put on a pair of Timbs for the occasion."

"Yeah, I can see. Their laced, too. You look like you coming straight out of the hood."

She crossed her arms across her chest, showing her disapproval. Noticing her ill grill, he had to come at her on some other shit.

"I have taken the week off. So, this is how I dress outside of the workplace. Do you like?" Devon asked, as he made a full circle.

"It's interesting."

Venus couldn't help to think that she liked this look better than the stuffy executive look he usually wore. He was undeniably gorgeous either way, but it was something about the way he looked now that made her pussy throb. She felt daring at this point. *Licking his earlobe wouldn't be too much, would it? Nah, he would probably take it as a sign of affection.*

Wanting him to know that his style was okay with her, she went in for the kill by gently pressing her tongue on his earlobe. He even tasted good.

"So, baby, what's up? You got a sister looking good, smelling good, feeling good for a nigga, and you got to do something important tonight? What's up with that? I thought maybe we could hang out. Go somewhere and get better acquainted."

Venus was not about to walk away without giving him something to think about.

Devon was completely lost in her words. Her scent was arousing him. His manhood was at attention again, bulging through his pants like a sword ready for war. He wanted Venus in the worse way. Taking her would be a violation, though. This was his brother's chick. He had to get it together before she changed his mind about his meeting. Then again, he wasn't about to betray his brother. That was a no-no.

"Vee, listen. You look so good you can make a nigga lose focus. Right now, I can't afford that, so maybe you can give me a rain check."

Devon noticed the pain across Venus's face. She was disappointed by his statement. He didn't want to make her feel bad. He just wanted to buy time. Six days is all he needed to get what he came for. Then Damion could come back to make his claim.

Sexy

Chapter 16

It had begun to rain, and Toy was still not at their meeting place. With only five minutes left, Devon hoped Toy hadn't caught punk fever on him. The clock was ticking, and time didn't wait for no one.

After his encounter with Venus, he had rushed over to Damion's crib to change up. It felt good rummaging through his brother's things. His twin had excellent taste in clothing. Devon looked for something casual, but the search didn't take long because he came up with zip, zero, nada. All of Damion's clothes were made for a businessman who worked a nine-to-five, not a thug who lived or died on the streets of New York.

Devon had made a mental note to bring this to Damion's attention. From the looks of it, Damion didn't have much of a social life, something that needed to be looked into. Although he wouldn't mind throwing on something from Damion's collection of the finest designer wear, nothing really seemed to capture the style he was looking for. The selection of suits, slacks, button-down shirts, and shoes was unbelievable—Brooks Brothers, Perry Ellis, Valentino, Dolce & Gabbana, Ralph Lauren, Bill Blass, and that's just to name a few. Damion was living large. Still, there was nothing casual enough for the occasion. As an afterthought,

Devon decided to just stop by the nearest Jimmy Jaz and pick up some hood gear. Being that it would be Toy's first time meeting Damion, what he wore really didn't matter.

Now dressed in green Army fatigues and black-on-black Timbs, Devon waited by the Hudson River off 125th Street. Toy had appeared from nowhere. Devon observed the surrounding area from a distance. One could never be too careful, especially with a trifling nigga like Toy. If he turned on Supreme, turning on him wouldn't mean shit. All Toy was concerned with was the paper he could make out of the deal. This was an 'every man for himself' game. Devon continued to watch Toy, as he crept up on him from behind. Toy spun around when he felt someone's hot breath on his neck. That's how close Devon got without being noticed. For a slight second, Toy thought he was starring into the eyes that could only belong to Devon. Toy was aware that Devon had a twin, but damn, the thought of two niggas looking exactly alike was scary.

"Damion?" Toy asked.

"Yeah…you Toy?"

"Yeah, what's good? Damn, if I didn't know any better, I would have sworn that you were Dee."

"Yeah, I know."

What Devon wanted to say was you should know better, but decided to play it safe and stick to the plan.

Devon reached into his pocket and pulled out a wad of bills, which totaled $25,000. Toy's eyes almost popped out of his head when he foolishly tried to grab the money out of Devon's hand. Devon pulled his arm back, away from Toy's reach.

"Not so fast, my brother. Before I give you what Dee promised, I need to ask you a few questions."

"Listen, your bro and I made a deal. Don't be tryin' to play me."

"Chill. I'ma give you what you came for. I just want to know if your word is good."

"Yeah, my word is good. I wouldn't have come this far. My word is all I got."

"Yeah, yeah, nigga, I've heard it all before. Your words don't mean shit if you ain't got no balls. You got balls, Toy?" Devon's devilish smile didn't go unnoticed.

Still looking at the cash Devon held in his hands, Toy replied, "Yeah, I got balls. Want to see them?"

"Alright, then let's get down to business."

Devon drilled Toy for all the information he could provide him on Supreme. Where did he live? Who was his right-hand man? Who was his latest head piece? If Supreme had a chick, Devon wanted to know all about her. She would be the weakest link in Supreme's operation. Toy's description of her was a rebel without a cause - a soldier. She was a Puerto Rican chick from the lower East Side, who used to come uptown to hang out with some of her people from the projects. This was where she had met Supreme. Now, she was a prisoner in her own home, so getting close to her would be the hard part.

Anywhere that Silky went, she was escorted by Supreme's bodyguards-clubs, beauty salon, shopping. If they could, they probably would escort her to the bathroom. From Toy's understanding, Silky didn't mind living this way. The benefits were worth it. In return for living in luxury, Silky had to live by the code, Supreme's code.

Devon sat in silence as Toy made that last statement. *Supreme's code - what the fuck did that mean?* By the time Devon finished with Supreme, his code would be broken. His code wouldn't mean a fucking thing where he was going—Hell!

Devon continued to pace in front of Toy as he started to describe Twista- the only man Supreme allowed himself to connect with. Supreme didn't trust many people, and he had good reason not to. The game had changed somewhere along the way, and the more money you had, the higher the risks.

You had hustlers snitching on hustlers now. It was bad business to have everyone up in yours.

Devon understood that better than anyone. Cutthroat motherfuckers made it known by way of attitude that they wanted you out of the way. The hustlers came a dime a dozen, but the fewer there were, the more the money. Nowadays, there were confidential informants on every set. Not only did these C.I.'s become part of someone's team, they were niggas a hustler would break bread with. There was a great risk with letting anyone get too close.

"The streets just aren't the same." Toy's expression was blank, but his mind was racing. The words that flowed from his mouth were real and so fucking true. Toy was risking his life for the information he was throwing at Dee. There was no room for error. If ever Supreme got wind that he was helping his worst enemy, a war would break out and he would surely be disposed of.

"Dey, are you sure you know what you're doing? Do you know what you are getting yourself into? This nigga Supreme has almost every single block from 96th Street to 125th Street on lockdown."

Devon got the sense that Toy was scared as shit of Supreme. Out of fear, Toy could turn the tables. Therefore, Devon had to make him feel secure. He couldn't afford for Toy to renege on him.

It was now past midnight. The temperature had dropped and the rain was heavier. It was finally time to move out. Devon and Toy drove around the neighborhood, while Toy pointed out all of Supreme's new spots. They watched the managers, runners, lookouts, as well as the base heads. Supreme was clocking major paper with the spots open 24-hours-a-day, seven-days-a-week. Devon studied all of the major players on Supreme's main spot, the spot that started it ALL—the Hole on 100th Street between Third Avenue and Lexington. That was where all of Devon's problems had begun.

He sat quietly and waited for a pickup to take place. He needed to get a good look at this dude Twista that Toy had told him about. Devon observed how the whole operation was being run. The dealers sold the dime bags of crack cocaine, and then handed the money over to the managers who would run up into one of the abandoned buildings. From the looks of things, inside one of the apartments is where the money was kept.

The product must be kept there, too, Devon thought, as he continued to analyze the operation.

There were two lookouts on the rooftops with what seemed to be Nextel walkie-talkies. There were two more lookouts stationed on each corner of the block. Toy told Devon that every eight hours Twista would come around to collect the funds. He would then disappear until the next pickup. No one ever knew how he would arrive—be it by car, bike, or on foot. All anyone knew was that his routine never changed. Like clockwork, every eight hours he would make his run. But he always appeared as if from nowhere.

Supreme was cautious. His soldiers were trained to observe and not trust. Fortunately, for him, Devon had also been trained by Supreme. And when trained by the best, you become one of the best—and if smarter, even better.

At that instant, Devon noticed a black Range Rover cruising down Third Avenue. Because of the tinted windows, he was unable to get a good look at the driver.

"Who's that?" Devon asked Toy, as he pointed towards the SUV.

Toy looked a bit confused, and then realized that the truck belonged to a guy from Washington Heights.

"Yo, that shit belongs to some nigga from up at the Heights!"

"What's his name, man?" Devon said, becoming aggravated with Toy's mellow response.

"His name is Lizard, bro. And chill! Don't be fuckin' barking at me. I ain't your son."

"Alright, alright. The nigga is all in the way, though."

"Yeah, I know. I ain't never seen that nigga on the East Side. Something must be going down."

Devon's face dropped. He knew exactly what was about to go down. Shit was about to hit the fan.

As the truck pulled up to the curb at 100th Street, all of the doors flew open. The Geechies climbed out, making it clear for Jaz to emerge onto the sidewalk.

Devon lowered himself, pulling Toy along with him.

"What's up, Dey? Who's that? Damn, that bitch look good than a motherfucka."

Devon turned around to stare at Toy as though he was the devil himself.

Jaz had gone straight back to her place after her meeting with her crew. She needed to talk to Devon about his situation with Supreme. Jaz didn't want to interfere without his knowledge. When she had reached the apartment and found that Devon had already hit the streets, Jaz called in the crew once again with the code they all knew so well -- 666. Then, she rushed into her bedroom, changed clothes, and hit the streets, too.

Now standing by the curb, Jaz was outright stopping traffic with her all-black leather Prada suit, black M.C. boots, and jet-black hair that was neatly corn rolled going back away from her face.

Devon felt like he was in another world. This shit couldn't be happening. He didn't want his mom out on the streets. But who was going to stop her? Once she made her mind up to do something, it was a wrap. He continued to watch Jaz as she reached for something his Uncle Lizard had passed off to her. It was a shiny object that she was now placing on her waistband.

"Yo, that chick is off the hook. Did you see that? That bitch got a lot of heart doing that shit right out in the motherfucking open."

"Shut the fuck up, Toy! I need to think."

"Think about what, yo? Supreme must have really fucked up. You know them uptown niggas ain't no joke. They don't play when it comes to their paper. Now he is going to get what he deserves—well, unless he gets them first," Toy said as an afterthought.

"You can say that again?" Devon tried to act as natural as possible. "Either way the nigga is doomed."

The Geechies entered the block and walked up to a group of young so-called gangstas that were hustling, while Jaz stood by on the corner with Trouble and Lizard. They looked like they were making casual conversation, but Devon knew better. The Geechies had been very much respected around the neighborhood because of their rep. Devon just hoped they weren't desperate enough to blow his cover. Supreme couldn't get wind that he was still alive. Devon needed Supreme to believe that Toy had actually killed him.

"There he goes, Dey," Toy hollered.

"Who?" Devon had lost focus on what he had come to do. Seeing his mother derailed his concentration.

"Twista, nigga! You better wake the fuck up."

"Where?"

"Right there walking on the downtown side with the brown leather trench."

Devon hurried to look at the target. He was surprised to find that Twista was dressed casually. Twista looked like the average Joe. The discipline that Supreme had instilled in his workers was what kept him in the game so long. Devon always wondered why Supreme had never gotten bagged. Now, while watching Twista move his way up the street, he knew. Everything they did was low key and in order—not like when Devon was on the streets with Supreme.

In the beginning, Supreme was obsessed with looking the part of a hustler. However, time and money had changed his way of thinking. Little did Supreme know that Devon was getting to know him all over again by observing his soldiers.

Sexy

Chapter 17

Twista couldn't take his eyes off the amazingly beautiful woman who stood on the corner. The curves of her body were saying something, but the swing of her jet-black hair was what really caught his attention. It was the attitude. Her style and demeanor made her the most exquisite creature he had ever laid eyes on. Her mere presence was that of a warrior. The way she stood by the curb in her no-nonsense pose captured his attention. She looked dangerously breathtaking.

He liked what he saw before him. Twista was lost in her sex appeal. He glanced in her direction several times, and then finally their eyes locked. *Damn those eyes are powerful,* Twista thought to himself.

Jaz didn't think much of the man before her until he made himself noticeable. He was shaking his head back and forth, as though fighting with himself. She suddenly got the strangest feeling that this nigga was one of Supreme's men.

Her gut never failed her in the past, so she ran with her first instinct.

Twista walked past her, but did not break eye contact. He didn't want to lose sight of her. He was planning to get her digits once he had made the pickup. Jaz was planning a more dangerous act as she held her stare.

Twista made his way to the entrance of one of the tenement buildings on 100th Street. Slowly, he passed some of the players who hung out or worked on occasion. But the stupid motherfuckers didn't notice him because they were too busy trying to get their mack on with some old Gs. Twista could remember when he was their age. He was pussy hungry, too—not sometimes, but all of the time. He laughed at the thought that pussy was pussy no matter what the age or color. Pussy just didn't have a face.

Twista entered the building through the basement. He had walked over to the steps that would lead him into the lobby, but he suddenly ducked down and disappeared. Once in the basement of the building, he walked over to the door that would give him entrance to the first floor. His destination—the second floor—where all of the work was being held. The building had been closed down by the City due to violations brought upon by the owner. The slumlord had lost his day in court, and now the City had taken ownership. This caused the families to move out until "they" (the City) decided to renovate or sell to some other real estate investor, who also wouldn't give a shit about the violation codes either. Until then, Supreme had taken over.

Up to the second floor Twista ran, making the transaction as smooth as possible—words need not be exchanged unless there was a problem. He threw the Nike gym bag over his shoulder and secured his .45 Magnum while skipping steps. He had arrived back in the basement in no time. However, just as he was about to emerge onto the street, the door was being blocked by the old Gs he had noticed earlier. He tried to back up slowly. In the darkness of the basement, he could see that the ladies in the shadows were moving forward in his direction.

He quickly squatted down, quietly placed the gym bag by his side, and removed his pistol from his waistband. Due to the lack of lighting, Twista had to squint. He became disoriented as the ladies moved in different directions—like rats looking to feed. Twista could hear their whispers, but nothing they said was clear. He didn't know who they were or what the fuck they wanted. He was sure about to find out, though.

One of the ladies called out to him, "Here, dawgy, dawgy. Come out, come out wherever you are."

The first voice cracked a little, but the second was much more in control.

"Come on, baby. We don't want to hurt you. We just came for what's in the bag."

The third voice was much softer. "You don't want to die for another nigga's paper, do you? It's not like he would give his life for you."

All of the voices were coming from in front of him now. He tried to move further away, but found himself with his back against the wall, or so he thought. However, there was somebody standing behind him, shoving a cold metal object against his skull.

"Didn't you know that there is no place to run? If a person wants you bad enough, they'll get you."

Jaz cocked her gun, and then placed it back against Twista's head. If need be, she would blow his fucking brains out. At the present moment, she was only thinking about what she had come for, and she was going to get it no matter what. The money would be the key to open up Pandora's Box (Supreme).

"What the fuck do you want? Why don't you just get to the fuckin' point?" Twista shouted, in hopes that one of the fellows outside would hear him.

"What's your rush, daddy? You got somewhere to go?"

Twista was getting irritated by the cat and mouse game they were playing. "What the fuck you going to do, bitch?"

"Bitch! I got your bitch," Jaz, always the easy one, whispered into his ear. "Lay down on the floor, playa playa. There is no need for you to get indignant."

Twista complied with the chick's orders. He lay face down on the cold, dirty, concrete floor, while still looking for a way out.

"Drop the gun while you're at it."

Twista hesitated for a slight second.

"Nah! I'm not going to repeat myself."

Twista released his grip, sliding the .45 in front of him. The shadows were directly on top of him now. He could hear them breathing.

Chyna picked his .45 up and pointed the weapon at him. "It be real fucked up if they found your ass down here shot up by your own shit." Chyna had been missing the adventure of the streets, but she wanted nothing more than to make Twista her come back. Laughing, she continued, "I have a message for your boss."

"My boss?"

Now he knew what this was all about. Those eyes on the chick by the curb, there was something about those eyes. Twista tried to go back to when their eyes had locked. Then without further ado, it hit him like a ton of bricks—those eyes on the chick were familiar. Those eyes belonged to Devon. Reality was setting in. The chick on the corner was Devon's mother, Jaz. He had fallen short of his awareness. Twista had allowed her beauty to distract him.

"Yeah, your boss, Tell him that he fucked with the right one now."

Chyna wanted to say more, but Jaz stepped into the dark and away from the scene. She had disappeared as quickly as she had appeared, walking off with $150,000 of Supreme's money. Now, Chyna had to get them out of there.

Chyna told Twista to count to one hundred while they stepped back out of the doorway and ran. Devon watched as the Geechies ran from the building and jumped into the waiting truck. He waited to see if his mother would come out next. She didn't.

Looking up and down the structure of the building, floor by floor, his eyes roamed. The fire escapes were all clear of human contact. He even searched the rooftops. Nothing!

Where the hell did she go?

He was becoming worried. He wanted to jump out of his ride, run up in the building, and look for her. Something stopped him, though. He figured if any of those stories were true, his mother had shit covered.

Jaz had grabbed the bag right from under Twista's nose and walked backward in the darkness, all the while looking into Chyna's eyes. She stood against the far wall closest to the staircase. That's where she took off her 3-1/2" Prada boots, removed a pair of cheap Bruce Lee Chinese shoes from the small of her back, and placed them on her feet. As quietly as possible, she continued stuffing the Prada boots into the bag with the money just stolen from Twista. Once the Geechies were out of the building, she walked silently up the stairs, avoiding any objects that might give her whereabouts away.

Twista was still lying flat on his stomach, counting. Jaz could hear the numbers blurted out in anger, as she reached the top of the stairs. All those years of working out had really paid off.

On the rooftop, Jaz jumped over the edge and onto the next building. The tenements on 100th Street were built right next to each other, making the crossover easy. She exited that building on Lexington Avenue, looking from side to side, making sure that the coast was clear.

When she saw that there was no one in sight, Jaz dashed toward the truck, leaped through the open door, and said, "On to the next spot."

Meanwhile, a few blocks over and a few hours or so later, Twista stood before the very pissed off Supreme. Supreme was so angry that his eyes were bloodshot red.

Twista didn't say a word. Even though they both hadn't said a word, Twista was fully aware of how Supreme operated. This could possibly be their last conversation. Supreme's anger wasn't just based on Twista's lack of ignorance. It was mainly because prior to Twista's return, Supreme had already received two phone calls from two of his spots claiming they were hit by a bunch of chicks. He was out of a great deal of money and someone had to answer for that.

"So what you're telling me is that you allowed yourself to get chumped by a bunch of broads, man?" Supreme had finally said.

"Nah, man."

Supreme listened attentively as Twista described the scenario. Nothing he said would make a difference. Supreme had already made up his mind long before Twista had arrived at his doorstep. Supreme wouldn't have been surprised if Twista had set the robberies up himself. If he didn't, well it was too bad. Twista was shit out of luck. Supreme didn't feel sorry for the underdog. Playas come a dime a dozen.

"Not just any broads, my man. It was that kid's mom."

Now that caught Supreme's attention. He jumped forward into Twista's face.

"What the fuck did you just say?"

Supreme was breathing so hard now that Twista thought the nigga was going to fall out.

"Yo, Sup, be easy."

"Be easy! Are you fuckin' crazy? Do you have any idea what the fuck you just said?"

Twista didn't respond.

With that news alone, Supreme was put back in his place.

Chapter 18

Feeling tired from a night of tossing and turning, Damion awakened to the sound of cell gates opening at six a.m. Live count is what they called the first count of the day. All inmates were required to stand by their cell doors. The point of this was to make sure all the inmates had made it through the night. Being that Damion was not aware of this procedure, he had received his first warning. He was not where he was supposed to be.

Just his luck—the midnight officer was one of those military types, running his block according to the little green book he carried in his back pocket. Although it was part of the job, some officers didn't bother with making their 30-minute routine rounds. Damion was grateful though that Mr. Taylor did. One never knew the dangers that lurked during those hours.

His pupils were dilated by the bright light, and the sound of the officer's voice startled him.

"Aviles, get up!" the officer screamed into the darkness.

"Yes, sir."

Damion jumped from the flat iron bed frame that caused his lower back to ache. *That bed is so damn uncomfortable,* he thought to himself. But, now was not the time to complain about it. He stood in front of the cell wearing a solid white pair of boxer shorts and a white wifebeater he had found among his brother's things. How he wished he had packed one of his silk boxers. The cotton material was really not his style.

"Don't make me have to tell you again! You know your ass is supposed to be by this fuckin' door!"

"Yes, sir," was all Damion could say, while wiping the sleep from his eyes.

There was no excuse, none that he (Mr. Taylor) would understand. What was he supposed to say—*Oh, excuse me, sir, but I didn't know. I am not who you think I am.* Yeah, right! Damion could never get use to living in a place like this.

After being counted like cattle, like a piece of meat at a meat factory, he stretched the muscles in his body. Once he was able to find relief, he immediately prepared for his day in the big house. The outside world was riding his nerves hard as he began to dress. He wondered what his brother was doing, how Venus was getting along, and he even thought about his mother. But that was another story altogether.

Damion had seen a look in her eyes he had never seen before; the look of pain and confusion. He was concerned and with good reason. He thought about Marcus, who was able to beat the disciplinary ticket he had received after the fiasco in the visiting room. He blamed the ordeal on his female visitor, causing her to be placed on his negative visiting list. Marcus was relieved of all charges and was being released from solitary confinement. Losing the V.I. wasn't any big deal to him because he didn't know the chick, so it wasn't any love loss. The plot was played out to perfection.

Damion dressed in a pair of State green pants that felt like cardboard against his skin, a button-down shirt from one of the many prison vendors, and a pair of Adidas shell toe. The message he had received from Marcus was to meet him at the Law Library. There, they would be able to talk without anyone overhearing their conversation.

Though he had arrived on time for his meeting with Marcus, Marcus didn't seem to notice. He was huddled over in a corner talking to someone. They were so deep into their convo that Marcus didn't realize that Damion had rolled up on him—not a good sign in a place like this. If he hadn't known better, he would have thought that Marcus and his companion sat together with their elbows on the wooden table, leaning in, looking into each other's eyes. The gesture would make anyone think that Marcus was a homo.

Damion immediately tried to erase those thoughts from his mind, although it wasn't uncommon. Homo thugs really did exist in this type of confinement, living in the shadows of the prison walls, giving in to the loneliness and finding comfort in the arms of another man.

He watched closely as Marcus continued to converse with his back towards him. Damion was able to feel the chemistry between the two. His image of Marcus was shattered in an instant.

Damion moved forward, grabbing a chair and sliding it close to Marcus, then sat down. Marcus turned his head to find Damion glaring at him with disapproval. If Damion could have burned a hole through him, he would have.

"Hey, nigga, what took you so long?" Marcus asked, as he tried to ease the moment.

"I've been here a minute. You just didn't notice."

"Yeah, well, it's all good. How you doing?" asked Marcus with a smirk on his face.

"I'm good," Damion responded—never once taking his eyes off the man in front of him.

There was something strange about him. Damion couldn't quite put his finger on it, so he continued to stare. There was something really weird going on.

"Yo, Dey. What's up with you, man? Why you lookin' like that?"

"Ain't nothing. Why?" His tone was angry with disgust. Then it hit Marcus.

"Oh, shit, nigga, you!" Marcus stopped short of what he was saying and began to laugh.

He couldn't control his laughter, holding onto his stomach as though his insides were going to burst. Tears even streamed down from his eyes.

"What the fuck is so funny?"

"Yo, nigga, you are buggin'." Marcus stood up, pointing directly at his companion. "Look at him real good, Dey. What do you see?"

"What the hell do you mean, 'what do I see'? That is a real stupid question."

"Just answer it, nigga. What do you see?"

Marcus now walked around to the back of Damion's chair, while Damion leaned in to get a closer look. Then he noticed the softness in the brother's brown eyes. That shit wasn't normal for a nigga. The lines around his face were deep with thought and embarrassment. His hair cut was short and tapered on the sides. It almost seemed that he processed the remaining strands with a relaxer, adding shine to produce the final touch. His skin at the base of his neck was soft, curving gently to expose two full-size breasts under a red and white football jersey. As Damion's eyes continued to roam, he noticed that he had on a pair of 501 Levi jeans, so tight that he could see the outline of a pussy.

Damion stood up, knocking over his chair. In shock, with his mouth wide open, it all registered. It was not a man that Marcus was all cuddled up with; it was a woman. His eyes moved back to Marcus, then back to the chick who sat there with her arms crossed over her breasts. Now, Damion waited for someone to say something or at least give him an explanation. Marcus instead took the opportunity to introduce his friend.

"Dey, this is Daija."

"Daija?"

"Yea, Daija."

* * * * *

She couldn't stop thinking about him. Today was her first day at her new job, and because things were slow at the moment, Venus just sat at her desk staring at the computer screen with the company's logo appearing every few seconds. She thought about how blessed she was by being hired after her second interview. That was cause for praise.

Venus had submitted her resume to some of the companies her parole officer had recommended. However, she never heard a word from them. Damion was the one who had suggested that she submit her resume to an up and coming record company by the name of Dirty Music Entertainment.

The CEO and founder of the label was a young man born in New York City but raised out in Tampa, Florida. Tampa is where he had discovered his talent for music. The kid was nasty with a beat, and when he mixed in his lyrics, he produced some of the best sounds in the South. David "Demonic" Negron was impressed with Venus as well as her resume. With the advice of his Mom/manager, he had decided to hire her as his personal assistant.

Venus picked up the phone and dialed Damion's cell phone number for the second time. She wanted to share her joy with him by taking him out for drinks. On the fourth ring, his voicemail picked up. She left another message asking him to return her call. She had great news to share with him.

Thoughts of their last meeting came into play. She could feel that something strange was going on. Damion had been so attentive when they were together, but lately, he seemed so distant. Venus understood that he was under a lot of pressure regarding his brother, but she still hoped for his attention. Maybe he needed time to sort things out. Dealing with the system (prison) on any type of level was stressful. No one knew that better than she did. She had lived it. Venus dialed his number again.

* * * * *

Devon listened to Jaz as she described how she got her hands on the cash that now lay stacked up on her dining room table. Her intention wasn't to keep the money. This was the only way to lure Supreme out of his cave.

"Mom, are you fuckin' crazy?"

"Yeah!"

"What do you mean, 'yeah'?"

Jaz reclined back in her chair and placed both hands behind her neck. She stretched and smiled before saying, "What do you want me to tell you, baby boy?"

Jaz continued to smile as she watched her son's face turn twenty different colors.

Devon had never wanted to involve his mother.

"You act like I wasn't able to handle this myself. Now the situation has taken another turn."

"You really didn't expect me to just sit around while my sons sacrificed their lives, did you?"

"Mom, I am not a little boy anymore. You need to take a good look at me and Dey. We are grown fuckin' men."

"Alright, son, I'm looking. Now what?"

"Now what! You tell me. You're the one who ran up on Supreme's spot. You robbed him of all this money, and you have the nerve to say, 'now what?'"

Devon was enraged. He was practically screaming at his mom. What he really wanted to do was wrap his hands around her throat and choke the shit out of her. Giving her a piece of his mind was not going to be enough. Jaz had crossed boundaries not even he could allow. He was a man, not some fucking two-year-old.

Jaz jumped up, looked him straight in the eyes, and said in a soft, low tone, "First and foremost, you need to know that my actions were not selfish. You say that you don't want me to get involved. Well, it's too late for that. Now get over it, and let's do what we got to do. We only have five days to get the information. We need to clear you of this murder charge. And we only got five fuckin' days to get my baby out of prison. Just five days to get our lives back. So, don't tell me not to get involved."

Devon didn't have words for her. The fire in her eyes was burning deep. She was beyond reach.

Sexy

Chapter 19

Devon checked his phone for messages. There were two missed calls, both from Venus. He listened to her sweet, sexy voice while taking his boots off and tossing them across the room. The sound of her voice was like music to his ears. After arguing with his mother for the past hour, Venus's voice was welcomed. She sounded like a cat in heat—urgent with a touch of lust. He pressed the redial button, and then waited for her to pick up on her end.

"Hey, baby." Venus always checked her caller I.D. beforehand, so she knew it was Damion before she even answered.

"Damn, girl. You sound like you're taking care of business—talking all sexy and shit."

"I wish I was. That's why I called you. I was hoping we could get together tonight."

"Oh yeah? What do you have in mind?" Devon asked, trying to remain in his brother's character. He knew he couldn't cross that boundary, but there was nothing wrong with having a little fun.

Devon lay back on his old bed with his back against the headboard. Some things had changed throughout the apartment, but his bedroom remained the same. It was exactly how he had left it when he moved out. His brother's side of the room was untouched, as well.

"Well, I got the job at Dirty Music Entertainment."

"Oh yeah? That's what's up!" Devon replied, although he had no idea what the fuck she was talking about, nor did he know what to say.

"That's what's up? You're the one that told me to send my resume in to them. That's more than just a simple 'that's what's up'. What's wrong with you, Dey?"

"Nothing."

"I thought you would be excited for me."

Venus's voice sounded bitter and disappointed. She had become vexed and used to sarcasm to show her disapproval for his lack of interest.

"Listen, Vee, I really don't know what it is you're expecting from me. I don't know what you're talking about, so your attitude is really uncalled for."

"What the fuck do you mean you don't know what I'm talking about?"

Silence.

"Hello, Dey. Are you still there?"

"Yeah!" Devon suddenly switched up on her. "Listen, Venus, I got to go."

Damion's sudden outburst hurt Venus. She thought he would have been happy for her. How wrong she was.

"Yeah, alright, whatever." Venus placed the phone back on its base.

At the other end, Devon snapped shut the cover to his celly, disconnecting the call with Venus. He felt bad for the way he treated her, but he had too many things on his mind. He wasn't about to entertain his brother's broad or any other broad for that matter. Women were the last thing he wanted to think about. Damion would just have to understand that he had much more important matters to take care of.

His mother had made shit complicated. Now he had to figure out how to clean up her mess. He thought his plan was much simpler than the shit that Jaz had pulled. His mother was off the hook.

He had to remain focused and change his strategy. Pussy wouldn't become a weak point in this factor, although he wouldn't mind getting into something right now. His dick craved the warmth of some chick's love canal. One thing he knew for sure was that when all of this was over, he would get up in some ass. He wouldn't switch back until he was completely satisfied. Devon wondered how his brother was getting along. He hoped that prison life wouldn't dramatize his ass, especially on the pussy tip.

* * * * *

The sun was setting. He watched as the citizens of New York City emerged from the train station on 116th Street and Lexington Avenue. Taking a bit of the pizza he had just ordered, he glanced at his watch. It was time.

As he walked east toward Supreme's brownstone, Toy observed his surroundings, making sure that he wasn't being followed. Once there, he waited patiently. He sweated profusely, wiping the sweat that ran off his forehead every few seconds.

Time was at a standstill as he stared at Supreme's windows. There had been no sign of life for a while behind the vertical blinds. Then, out of nowhere, Toy noticed that a light was switched on. Toy had discovered through word of mouth that Supreme had turned his nights into days and days into nights. When the sun went down, Supreme woke up. When the sun came up, Supreme slept—a true hustler's lifestyle; a predator—like an animal that preys upon others to make its fortune. Everyone involved in this scheme would have to train their bodies as well as their minds to do the same.

Earlier in the day, Damion had called a meeting between Toy and himself. He wanted to tell Toy that there had been a change of plans. It was short notice. However, if executed correctly, nothing would go wrong. Toy looked at his watch every few seconds while he waited for the sun to go down completely. Fear crept up on occasion, especially when he thought about Damion and the way he described the Geechies, his mom, and his aunt Trouble. After hearing how Damion's family got down, Toy realized that he was way over his head and knee-deep in shit. Things were about to get real ugly in the hood.

Most importantly, if things didn't go according to plan, they could all wave their freedom goodbye. The risk of what they were about to do was great—possibly making a New York State correctional facility their permanent address. That is one place Toy was not willing to return to. This was his last chance at getting some major paper and bouncing.

He thought about his people down South that wouldn't mind helping him start his life over. Toy was tired of the game. Most of all, he was tired of all the bullshit that went along with it. The game didn't leave a nigga shit but prison or death—a true reality. Getting the fuck out of New York was the best idea he had come up with, and it was getting sweeter by the minute.

Toy reached for his cell phone, and dialed the code that Damion had asked him to use once he was in position and the target had risen.

For hours, Devon sat in a corner watching his mother and Aunt Trouble as they made several trips to Trouble's basement. Lizard had purchased the three-bedroom, two-bath house for Trouble shortly after her accident. He wanted nothing more than to bring Trouble into a safe environment—away from the hood and her old life. He wasn't willing to risk her safety for nothing in the world. He had promised her while she lay sleeping on her hospital bed that he would forever take care of her. And he did.

By making the transition as easy as possible, Lizard had looked at several properties in the area of New Rochelle,

New York. He thought about moving up further, but nevertheless settled for Westchester County. He needed someplace central—a place where he would be able to get to the city at a second's notice. Although he had chosen to move Trouble out to the suburbs, he would never give up his own business. The hustle was in his blood. New Rochelle had become the perfect location to suit their individual needs.

With each trip that Trouble made, she handed Jaz two or three wooden crates. When she decided that ten crates would be enough, Jaz began to open each one with the fork side of a hammer. Carefully, she lifted the tops, motioning her son to come stand beside her.

Devon's mouth fell open when he saw what was inside. It was unbelievable. Each crate contained two pistols of every size and make. As he took inventory, he counted twenty guns altogether—four 9mm, three .45 Magnums, two .38 specials, two ivory-handled 22s, two sawed-off shotguns, five Uzis, and last, but not least, there were bullets for each and every one. They had all captured his attention, but the .38 specials were the ones that really stood out. They looked like the guns the NYPD used back in the late 80's and early 90's. They reminded Devon of the rumors he had heard so long ago.

The rumor was about two detectives and how they came up missing while investigating a drug empire that was located on 110th Street—an empire that his mother Jaz and Aunt Trouble had built. Devon began to believe that these rumors weren't mere rumors anymore. They were factual stories based on Jaz's past. Nothing else would surprise him at this point.

As darkness shadowed the city like a soft blanket, Trouble removed the weapons from their resting place, laying them out across her dining room table. Upstairs, the rest of the ladies, Chyna, Cookie, Lissy, Evelyn, and Tima were putting on their kick-ass gear. Once ready, they moved smoothly and easily down the steps. The look on their faces had transformed from loving and caring aunts to both Devon and Damion to outright gangsters ready to do some damage. It was time to move out.

He couldn't help but to notice how good they looked in their all-black attire—with their military cargo pants all tight and snug, exposing every inch of their curves. They also wore black full-piece leotards that left nothing to the imagination. Hair was worn back in tight corn rolls, showing only the tips where length wouldn't allow them to tuck under a NYPD baseball cap.

The disguise was to modify the appearance. There was always someone watching on the streets of Spanish Harlem. Nevertheless, the point was to trick any nosey onlookers.

"You guys already know what needs to be done," Jaz said, as she began to issue the burners along with the ammunition.

Jaz had already selected two for herself. So, it was open house for the Geechies as they grabbed, handled, and selected their weapon of choice. Devon stood close by with an intense look on his face. Dazed at their movements, with only the sound of weapons being cocked back into position, they all said, "Yeah!" breaking the trance.

* * * * *

Venus had waited a while for a return call from Damion. After realizing he was not going to call back to apologize, she took an early lunch break. Venus jumped on the #6 train heading towards Washington Projects. She refused to go unnoticed. Damion was going to have to give her an explanation one way or the other. His outburst was unnecessary.

Exiting at 103rd Street and Lexington Avenue, she walked quickly down the street. Beating the lights and traffic, she approached Damion's mother's building—just in time to see Damion leaving.

Venus suddenly stopped short to hide behind a narrow tree. She watched him as he looked from side to side, as though waiting for someone to jump out at him. He seemed nervous—in a rush was more like it. Damion walked across the parking lot in long strides. His right hand coming up beside him, he pointed his automatic ignition key and made his truck come to life. When he opened the driver's side door and climbed in, Venus ran across the fenced in lawn, climbed over a 12-inch fence, and ran across the street to hail a cab.

"Follow that Lexus," Venus yelled at the cabbie.

"What?"

"Follow that fuckin' truck," she demanded, pointing in its direction while holding a hundred dollar bill in her hand.

The driver didn't argue with her once he saw the money thrown his way. Money talked and bullshit walked.

Sexy

Chapter 20

Now, standing outside of the Trouble's home, Venus hadn't realized how much time had passed by. She glanced at her watch. It had been three hours since her arrival. Venus peeked through the window. She couldn't believe her eyes; the women, the guns, and the whispers between them. Devon, who she still thought was Damion, stood on the sideline, while the women geared themselves up like the famous swat team.

Venus felt a sense of excitement run through the very core of her. She wanted nothing more than to knock on the front door and make her presence known. She considered the consequences of that more, and then thought against it. However, she continued to look through the window with anticipation. Venus tried to figure out through mere street knowledge what the hell they were up to.

Unsure, yet possessive of Damion, she tried to figure out what part he played in all of this. It was a surprise to her that Damion would be involved in this type of activity. He never once showed a thuggish side to him. Venus liked the man she saw through the window. The excitement she felt reached spots Damion knew nothing about yet.

She felt the moistness between her legs as she daydreamed of riding him. She wiggled her thighs as the wetness seeped through to her silk panties. Her pussy began to throb as she undressed him with her eyes. Venus imagined how good it would feel to have her legs wrapped around his broad shoulders while he stroked his manhood inside of her.

She watched as he backed up against the wall and placed his hand over his groin. He must have gotten excited, too, because he had a mean hard-on. Venus could see it through his black Ecko sweatpants. The bulge was one that would make any woman proud. He was truly blessed. Damion's jewels were something she wouldn't mind devouring one day, all day.

Devon felt a little uncomfortable. He sensed a presence lurking nearby. It felt as though someone, an outsider, was watching him. Looking from side to side, he tried to shake the feeling, but to no avail. Since his escape from Sing-Sing he hadn't felt paranoid, until now. He walked over to the front windows, swung the drapes to the side, and peeked out. The streets of New Rochelle were deserted, and the neighborhood was quiet. Devon thought for that slight second that when all of this was over, he would purchase a place out here, too, find a good woman, and settle down.

His outlook on life had changed so much since the day he had to pull the trigger. Although it was done to protect his brother, taking another life had really affected him. Not once did he regret the choice he had made at the moment. It was either his twin or the nigga who laid out by the curb. Twenty-five years was a small price to pay for his brother's life.

Devon continued to scan the street. To the right of him, he noticed a small shadow, a small figure losing balance and falling backwards onto the ground. He watched quietly as the person stood up, then brushed away at its clothing. Devon had turned around just in time to see his mom and the rest of the crew head towards the front door.

"Wait!" Devon hollered at Jaz. "Shhhh," he whispered, while placing his finger up to his lips.

Jaz turned around so fast at the sound of her son's voice, she almost snapped her neck.

"What the fuck," is all she could say.

She stared at him and saw something in his eyes, a warning. She knew that look anywhere. Jaz held her hand up at the Geechies, asking them to be easy.

Devon walked up to Jaz slowly, then removed one of the 9mm's she held in her waistband. He walked through the foyer and into the backroom where the second entrance to the house was located. Devon quickly opened the door and then stepped out. Turning the corner to look up and down the side of the house, he found the intruder. He could not believe the nerve of this broad. His mind went in different directions. He stood stuck as he looked at Venus. She was still trying to get herself together after falling and busting her ass.

"That's what the fuck you get for being so fuckin' nosey."

"Oh shit," Venus said, as her eyes almost jumped out of her head. She had been busted.

"Oh shit, my ass. What the fuck are you doing here?" Devon was now standing over her. "Don't even think about it." Devon grabbed her arm as she tried to run.

"Ouch! You're fucking hurting me, Damion." Venus struggled to release his grip.

"You haven't begun to feel real pain yet."

"Okay, okay. Get off of me."

"What the fuck do you think you're doing here, Vee?"

Shattered by the look on Damion's face, Venus was at a loss for words. For the first time in a long time, she had nothing to say. Venus had come to the conclusion that anything she said at this point would only make matters worse. She had fucked up royally.

Devon felt violated. He would never tolerate this type of behavior from any of his chicks, and he definitely was not going to tolerate it from Damion's.

Sexy

Chapter 21

Damion walked silently across the yard, listening to Marcus's description of his relationship with Daija. His mouth fell open when Marcus went on to say that Daija was his boo. She had begun to work for the Department of Corrections shortly after Marcus was handed his sentence. Searching through the internet, Daija had come across an employment service that supplied qualified individuals with a job for D.O.C. Conveniently, there was an opening at Sing-Sing for a legal assistant. Her short hair and men's clothing was just part of the disguise to hide her true identity. Under all of the baggy gear, Daija had a body to die for.

Daija would have done anything to be at her man's side and still would. Playing the role of a dyke became second nature to her. When she first approached Marcus with the idea, he was against it. His troubled eyes looked her up and down, and he asked her if she was crazy. Her answer was, "Yes, for you." Daija had made up her mind long before he had a chance to agree. His words went unheard.

Fortunately, things had worked out for the both of them. Marcus received luxuries the other inmates were not allowed. Daija received eight hours of pure ecstasy. Occasionally, Marcus would surprise her with a long session of deep stroking or a little head before she left for the day.

The risks of getting caught were well worth it. She couldn't see her life without him, not even for one second, even if it meant losing her job or maybe being convicted for fraternizing with state property. The thought of that happening made their episodes much more intense.

Both men walked over to the bench press, where Marcus positioned himself on the bench and then asked Damion to spot him while he lifted the 200-pound weights. This was one of Marcus's favorite pastimes, that and fucking his woman from time to time. A nigga couldn't get it any better. Fuck the homemade food and anything else Daija would try to spoil him with. It was the pussy he looked forward to.

Pushing 200 pounds above his chest, Marcus's body began to swell. After several reps, he lifted himself up and stood completely still as he tried to catch his breath. Damion thought this would be the perfect opportunity to get to know Marcus better.

"Yo, Mar, what do you plan on doing once you get out of here?"

"Me? I never really thought about it. I know one thing. This shit here is played the fuck out. Ain't nothing like getting some pussy without having to watch your back all the time." Marcus made the comment with a slight grin on his face.

"Yeah, I know. But, seriously, you need to start planning out your future."

"Why, Dey? You got something in mind?"

"Maybe. That depends on what you're interested in, what skills you may have, and what you are willing to do and not do."

"Dey, check it. Let me keep it real with you. I ain't ever thought about going legit. The streets and the game is all I know. Ever since my sister went away on a murder charge, my life has never been the same. Don't get me wrong. I'm not using that as an excuse. Well, maybe. Let's just say that she was everything to me." Marcus sighed while walking over to a picnic table.

"I didn't know you had a sister," Damion responded, surprised that Devon never mentioned it.

"You don't know much about me. Devon doesn't even know I have a sister, or any other siblings for that matter."

"Why not? I thought you two were tight?"

"We are. If we weren't, I would have never helped him get to where he had to go, feel me?"

"Yeah, I feel you."

"Anyway, we never really talked about home and family because it hurts too much."

"I hear you. Well, we don't have to discuss this shit right now. Just do me a favor."

"What's that?"

"Think about your future, man. I know I can help you out if you ever decide to turn your world around. I could probably get you a gig up in my people's club as a bouncer or something."

Damion gave Marcus some dap, then changed the subject.

Damion had so much to be grateful for. Not too many brothers in the system had much to look forward to once they hit the streets. About 99.9% of them would go back to the streets because they knew nothing else. Damion was going to make sure Marcus didn't fall into that category. He owed him that much. Damion thought about it as they walked back towards their blocks and made plans to meet again the next day.

While back in his own space, Marcus thought about the knowledge Damion was kicking at him. He reached for the photo he had stashed long ago. In it, Venus was much younger and so full of life. Her smile was unlike any he had ever seen. The smile was that of a mother caring for her child. The child was him, but Venus was not the mother. She was the sister who had become his mother when their mother turned to drugs and the streets.

Marcus would always be indebted to his sister for being there for him, and for never allowing B.C.W. to take him away. He closed his eyes as the memories flowed through his mind. Slowly, he brought the picture up to his lips, kissed her face, and replaced the photo. Vowing to one day see his sister again, his thoughts drifted to Damion's offer. He was seriously considering making changes in his life. A new life was exactly what the doctor ordered. Marcus was getting tired of doing the same old shit and getting the same results. If he planned on going to see Venus, he had to go correct.

Suddenly, he bent down by the side of his bed and reached for the cardboard box he had filled with books. He found exactly what he was looking for—a G.E.D. book he had borrowed from the school building. Although he had thought about getting his G.E.D., he never once opened the book. Marcus had fallen short; his confidence was at an all-time low at the time. Now, he was more than ready.

He opened the book and turned the pages. As he read a little of each chapter, he realized that he was capable of passing the test if he studied hard and applied himself. There was no better time than the present. Venus would be so proud to know that he didn't waste his time in the P-Nile.

From past conversations with her, she had made it clear that no matter where they were in life, education was the key—the one true freedom they needed so desperately. The thug life was played the fuck out. It was time for a new beginning.

* * * * *

Damion couldn't get through. The phone just rang and rang. Jaz always had her cell phone on and in near reach. He was concerned with not getting a response. Her voicemail wasn't even connecting. He tried one last time, and then decided to call his Aunt Trouble's numbers. She would know his mother's whereabouts. The phone just rang at her place, too. Something was going on; he could feel it in his gut.

Lock down was at ten p.m., and he wanted to get through to his people before he was locked in his cell for the night. Because Devon hadn't connected with him in any way, Damion was skeptical. Having to live the next twenty-one years behind these walls scared the shit out of him.

Damion tried one last time, but this time, he tried his own phone number. Right before his voicemail picked up, he heard his brother scream into the receiver, "This better be good, Dey!"

Damion's sigh of relief was heard in his tone when he answered his brother. "Damn, you can at least sound like you're happy to hear from me."

"I am, I am, but this stupid bitch of yours is ill, man." Devon held the phone close to his ear and walked over to the side, as the Geechies began to surround Venus. "I told you before I didn't have time to baby-sit," Devon whispered, still trying to cover for Damion's whereabouts.

"What the fuck are you talking about, Dee?"

"Your chick, man. She followed me out to New Rochelle, man. We getting ready to make some moves and your chick showed up at Trouble's crib. She didn't even have the fuckin' decency to knock on the door. The bitch was spying on me through the window. Where the fuck you find this fool anyway?"

Damion began to laugh uncontrollably. He found Venus's actions mad funny.

"What the fuck are you laughing at?"

"You, nigga. I forgot to tell you that my girl wasn't a pushover. The chick got game, a real trooper, a ride-or-die bitch. Whatever it is that you are planning, trust and believe me, she'll be down for whatever."

"So what you're saying is to put her down."

"That's completely up to you, son. Trust me, Dee, she's the one." Damion continued to laugh as he disconnected their phone call.

Devon was left holding the phone to his ear. The only sound he heard was a dial tone.

Devon looked over his shoulder at Venus, who was standing in the middle of the living room floor, her eyes glaring at all of the women with admiration. There was nothing gullible about her. There was no sign of fear whatsoever. Devon tried to read her. He wasn't sure if she was willing to be down or if she just wanted to get the fuck out of there. There was only one way to find out.

He walked in between Jaz and Trouble, stared deep into her eyes, and tossed his .45 Magnum at her. Both of her arms reached up and caught the piece between her hands. She held it straight up in front of her, pointing it directly at Devon's chest. All was said and done with that move. Fifteen years behind the walls was now nonexistent to her. In a matter of seconds, Venus had transformed into someone she never knew existed. Never once thinking about the pain she endured from her incarceration, Venus had committed herself at this point.

Jaz stepped up to Venus, took the gun from her hand, then instructed the Geechies to set her up. While Venus changed into her gear, Jaz informed her of their plan and what part she would play.

"As long as everyone follows my instructions to the letter, nothing will go wrong. Do you understand?" Jaz asked her, as she handed her a small .22 caliber pistol with an ivory handle.

"Yes!"

"Okay, don't fuck it up. It will cost you." Jaz turned her attention back to the Geechies. "Ladies, are we ready?"

Everyone nodded their heads.

"Okay, let's move out." Jaz was the first to lead the way.

Chapter 22

Toy spotted the SUV as it pulled up to the curb. He counted eight bodies in all when they emerged onto the sidewalk. Toy was not expecting one more person to be involved. Devon, who Toy still thought was Damion, told him that seven women, including himself, would be performing the takeover. So who the fuck was the broad running across the street and up the steps to Supreme's front door? Most importantly, what the hell was she wearing? He did not appreciate things changing without being notified. Now he had to look out for one more person. He really didn't need this shit.

While Venus ran to the front door, the Geechies ran towards the alley. Jaz motioned for Tima and Evelyn to climb the fire escape. They both crawled up the side of the building like cats, being extremely careful not to make noise. One false move and they could all be discovered. Once they reached the top, Tima looked over the side, then waved to let Jaz and the others know they were in position.

Jaz motioned the next set of Geechies, Cookie and Lizzy, to break through the basement lock with a small electric saw. It was amazing how quickly the Geechies had gotten it done. She was impressed. After all these years, they still had the skills to perform.

Time was of the essence. Jaz had estimated that the job would take about fifteen minutes. It was plain to see that they would accomplish their mission successfully. With two Geechies on the top floor and two Geechies on the ground floor, Jaz, Trouble, and Chyna entered the brownstone through the basement.

Devon allowed several seconds to pass before he drove up the block, parked the truck, and went down the alleyway to meet Toy.

Supreme was eating his breakfast of sunny side up eggs, toast, and a power shake, when his most loyal companion began to growl. Cypress didn't fuss much unless something was out of pocket. For years, Supreme thought his Rottweiler had a sixth sense. Trained only by Supreme, Cypress turned out to be his most valued assistant. That's why Cypress was rewarded with the best. Sometimes, Cypress had it better than any human could think possible. A T-bone steak for breakfast was a small price to pay for his loyalty. Cypress was priceless.

Supreme stopped midway through his breakfast to stare at his dog. Cypress had begun to pace the dining room floor. Motionless, Supreme listened carefully. There was nothing but silence throughout the house.

"What's up, boy?" Supreme asked his loyal companion in a whispered voice. "Is there someone out there?"

Cypress was now sitting in front of Supreme with his ears at attention.

Supreme pushed his chair back. He lifted himself up from the table and then walked quietly toward his office, the room where he had negotiated some of his biggest deals. The drug game had become very competitive, and niggas wanted Supreme out of the picture. His cheddar was long. His connection never failed him. Keeping the merchandise flowing was the biggest and most important part of the game. Some niggas couldn't eat right as long as Supreme had the streets on lock. That's the reason he had built the inside of his house like a fortress. Cameras faced every angle of the alleyways.

Now sitting back on his black leather swivel chair, Supreme looked into his security cameras. The monitors showed no sign of life outside of his brownstone. However, that didn't stop Cypress from growling towards the windows. If someone was out there trying to get at him, he would have to use his hidden passageway to escape. No one in their right mind would get this close to only rob him, so this meant that they were there to murder him.

Toy and Devon pointed a set of beam lights at Supreme's office window. Hoping to distract Supreme, they moved the beams from side to side, causing Cypress to go crazy, leaping and barking frantically. Supreme ran towards the windows, tossing the curtains to the side. He looked up and down the block in search of the intruder. Suddenly, he heard the front door.

The bells chimed loudly, causing Supreme to run over to his desk, where he dialed Twista's number.

"Yo, I'm being raided, I think."

"You think?" Twista yawned as he asked the question.

"Yeah, nigga. I think the motherfuckin' po-po or something is out front. Get your ass over here and check it out."

"Alright, man. I'm on my way."

Twista shut the celly off, and turned over on his side to find a fine chocolate sista snuggling up close to him. "It was some night, girl, but business calls. I got to go."

Memories of last night's episode caused Twista to get an instant erection. Thoughts on how Rome had wore his ass out drifted through his mind. He would have loved to stay and continue to serve her some of his long, deep strokes, but that would have to be put on hold.

Twista took his time as he showered and dressed. He wasn't about to hurry on Supreme's account. Twista was getting tired of jumping to every command Supreme shouted out. Besides, it probably wasn't that serious, just Supreme being paranoid again.

Ever since the spots were hit, Supreme had been out of control. He believed that it was an inside job. Someone in the family hated on him; someone on his team had set him up. Twista was tired of hearing the same old shit. All of the outbursts had made it hard for Twista to deal with.

Twista had also noticed that, on several occasions, Supreme would look at him with a twisted grill. Supreme never had to say a word; it was written all over his face that he didn't trust Twista anymore. So, if he didn't trust him, why the fuck was he calling him? Then something else came to mind as he dried, lotioned, and spread his clothes out across the bed.

Maybe with Supreme locked up nice and cozy somewhere, Twista could take over and make a name for himself. He would no longer be walking in Supreme's shadow. He would be the man and make someone else his bitch. Maybe that's exactly what Supreme needed— a reality check.

As Twista put the final touches on, he looked back towards the bed. Again, his dick became rock hard as he imagined climbing back in Rome's sweet ass. The thought of stroking her tight pussy caused him to remove all of his clothes and dive in. Supreme would just have to hold it down on his own. Supreme could wait. If not, fuck it. Twista would get there when he got there.

"Come here, girl, and show me that thing again. Yeah, baby, you know that thing when you climbed on it and... yeah, that's it."

Twista zoned out, forgetting Supreme's call ever came through.

Over and over, the bell rang. The beaming light was still shining and Cypress continued to bark. Supreme tried to wait it out, but the noise was getting to him. He decided to just walk over to the front door. He looked out of the French doors and saw someone standing there. If it had been the police, they would have come crashing through already. Maybe it was one of the neighbors.

"Who is it?" Supreme asked, when he realized it wasn't the cops but a chick laced in a full-length mink coat.

It was a black sable to be exact. Supreme recognized the quality immediately. He had attended enough fur shows to know that this chick had paper.

The chandelier earrings she wore sparkled against the fur, causing the skin on her face to glow. Her neckline was thin and smooth. The diamond necklace that encircled her neck hung low, touching the outline of her breast. Exquisite was the only word he could think of to describe the woman, who reached up with her small manicured hands to ring the bell once again.

Supreme didn't bother to ask who it was this time. Why even go there? From the expression on Venus's face, he felt that something was seriously wrong with her. Wanting to know what was going on, he opened the first set of doors, while signaling Cypress to tone it down.

Venus heard the door unlock. She had never played the role of a damsel in distress before, so all of this would be new for her. She just hoped she could pull it off. She took a deep breath, and then looked into his eyes. *Damn, this nigga looks good,* she thought, as the rest of her words flowed from her lips.

"Damn, baby, I thought you would never open this door. What took you so long?" Venus spoke quickly and reassuringly, as she pushed her way into Supreme's home. She continued to talk, making her way into the living room. Venus did everything in her power to make it seem as though Supreme knew her. "Well, why are you standing there looking crazy, baby? Hurry up and close the door. We need to talk, and we need to talk now."

Supreme was dumbstruck. He closed the door behind him. He watched as she walked into the living room, and then threw herself onto his leather sectional sofa. Supreme couldn't break the connection between his eyes and her thighs. Her coat had fallen open from the waist down, exposing a set of mouthwatering legs. He licked his lips as he and Cypress stood at the entrance of the living room, stuck.

Who the fuck is she and where the fuck did she come from, is all Supreme wanted to know. And he was about to find out.

Chapter 23

Step by step, Jaz made her way through the basement. Observation was one of Jaz's main skills, so she used that to her advantage. To the right of them, they found a 70-inch big-screen color TV with a built-in projector. Directly across was a soft leather sectional with throw pillows set neatly across its frame. Softly, she continued forward, where she found a pool table and a built-in bar with bar stools covered in a black-and-white zebra print. Apparently, this was Supreme's playroom, the place where he entertained.

Finally coming to the stairwell that would lead her up to the main floor, Jaz took a deep breath. With Trouble and Chyna closely behind her, Jaz felt confident. However, there was something nagging at her. Maybe it was the fact that she had been out of this life a long time, and having to get back into it was a little scary.

She opened the door slowly and, from a distance, she could hear Venus's voice. From the sound of things, everything seemed to be going according to plan. Venus was in. Jaz could also hear Supreme's breathing, slow and steady, or was it the beast that stood closely by its master's side.

Jaz opened the old wooden door wider, praying it wouldn't creak, and then stuck her head out slightly. She needed to make sure everything was clear before she allowed

Trouble and Chyna to follow. Her first view was of Venus, who was now standing by the bay windows where Devon and Toy watched from the street. Jaz continued to look silently as the Geechies made their way down from the third and second floors. This meant they were through with searching the rest of the house. It was obvious that Supreme was home alone. Once together on the main floor, they pulled out their weapons. It was now time to undo what was done by Supreme. It was now or never.

Venus continued to speak to Supreme as though they were old acquaintances. Although her tone had softened, Supreme was fully aware of her presence.

"What's wrong with you? You're lookin' at me as though I'm a stranger."

Venus opened her mink coat slightly, exposing herself yet again. Supreme could tell by all of the skin that was revealed that the woman standing before him had very little clothing underneath. That had definitely caught his attention. He also noticed her garter belt, which held her sheer silk stockings in place along with an ivory-handled .22 caliber pistol. The weapon was just as exquisite as she was, delicate and beautiful, sensitive but criminal.

Supreme searched his memory bank. *Where do I fuckin' know her from,* he asked himself, while taking a few steps closer. Maybe something would register if he got a better look.

"Come on, baby. I know you couldn't have forgotten me," Venus sang out, while licking her bottom lip.

Venus felt her chest tighten. Fear of what might happen if she couldn't pull this off overwhelm her. His eyes stared her down, deeply. What if she wasn't capable of answering all of the questions that were running through his mind? She had to get herself together and fast. All of their lives depended on her giving a great performance.

Venus started to regret getting involved in all of this bullshit. Thoughts of guards slamming cell doors and

166

disgusting prison food suddenly came to mind. Venus had allowed herself to get caught up in the rush. Watching Damion's people had brought a sense of excitement and adventure into her boring, pathetic life. She had forgotten all of the pain she had endured while at Bedford Hills. And now, in seconds flat, she risked going back.

Venus took a good look at what she was capable of still doing in the name of love. She promised herself at that moment that once this was all over, she would remove herself from Damion's life. Nothing was worth going back to the hell that waited behind the walls.

Back in the now, Venus continued to talk quickly, desperately trying to convince Supreme that they had met before. That was supposed to be the easy part. It was what the Geechies were planning to do to him that really scared the shit out of her.

Outside of the brownstone, Devon and Toy watched as Venus walked towards the window. She had moved the velvet drapes over to the sides, and then looked in both directions. She slowly turned back towards Supreme after letting Devon know that everything was everything. Venus continued to entice him with her sex appeal, applying a little flavor to the game.

"So, baby, tell me, when were you going to call? That night at Club Ecstasy, you led me to believe that it was going to be all about me and you."

Venus strolled towards Supreme in a cat-like gesture. When she finally found herself in front of him, she gently reached out to touch him with her freshly manicured nails.

Supreme was lost. He wanted to tell her that he had no fucking idea what the hell she was talking about, but couldn't find the words, or his vocal cords for that matter. His loyal friend wasn't moved, though. He sensed there was something wrong. Cypress began to growl again, as Venus got closer into Supreme's face. Being snapped back into reality, Supreme patted Cypress on the head and told him to be easy.

"Down, boy," Venus said, while trying to maintain her composure, not wanting her voice to sound shaky.

Suddenly, Cypress leaped forward, attacking Venus. He had gone straight for her throat, but got a hold of her mink collar. Cypress locked jaw and refused to let go. He growled viciously while he tugged and pulled at Venus.

Jaz heard the screams. The agony coming from Venus's cries altered the Geechies all at once. Jaz had to do something quick. The Geechies didn't wait for Jaz to hand out any orders. They were the first ones to enter the room.

Pop...pop...pop!

Someone had let off three shots. Cypress released his grip, and then collapsed onto his side.

Supreme went ballistic. It had taken him a minute to realize what the hell was going on around him. He had been so into Venus, with her charisma and her power to please and attract, that he had no idea there was anyone else in his house. The thought of being set up by this bitch caused him to dive forward, knocking her to the ground. Supreme crawled away from where the shots were fired, pulling Venus along with him.

"Get the fuck off of me." Venus struggled against the frame of his body.

"Shut the fuck up, bitch, before I blow your brains out."

Once behind the sofa, Supreme placed one of his hands underneath and found the built-in compartment he had installed for situations like this. He pressed a button and released the hatch. Its door popped open, and a tray holding two sawed-off shotguns slid out. He grabbed one and pressed the nose of the weapon into Venus's head.

"Chaos is about to break off in this motherfucker if you try anything," Supreme screamed over his shoulder.

Venus also screamed into the open air, "Don't shoot, please."

Together, they sat still and waited for their next move.

Outside, Devon continued to watch the brownstone. There was a slight movement behind the drapes, yet there was no indication whatsoever that there was any danger lurking between the stone brick walls. Hard as it may be to believe, he sensed his mother's presence, an immediate nearness. There was something going on.

He glanced down at his watch. It was one minute over their calculation. His mom was supposed to be in and out in fifteen minutes, not a minute longer. Anything over that, he was to go in with guns smoking.

Devon couldn't move, though. Something unnatural was stopping him. He couldn't put his finger on it, but there was something definitely off beam. It was as though something or somebody was holding his body down. Devon looked over at Toy for support, but he was staring at the brownstone mesmerized. Devon tried to shake the feeling. He focused his attention back to the situation at hand.

"Hey, Toy," Devon whispered.

"Yeah, what's good, Dey?"

"Something ain't right."

"Yeah, I know. You ready to do this?"

"I'm as ready as I'm ever going to be. My main girl is in there."

Devon and Toy crossed the street like two warrior soldiers ready for war. Devon climbed the brownstone's steps first, then waved Toy to follow. Together, they stood on each side of the front door with their backs against the wall. Devon rang the doorbell. There was no answer. He placed his ear against the door. It was too quiet. There was no sound coming through.

Worried that something was going on inside, he began to pound the door with his fist. Still nothing. Before he was able to pound on the door again, two shots rang out. His reaction was limited due to the fear of getting busted again and the fear of not being able to get back in time to get his brother out. Devon threw his body against the door with much force. He thought of Jaz who was inside trying to prove a point, the point being that no one fucked with her sons. He felt the same way. No one fucked with his moms.

Again, he threw his body against the door, but this time, he didn't need to use force. The door was opened by an unknown stranger.

"Who the fuck are you?" Devon questioned, pressing his glock into the gentleman's face.

"It's okay, baby!" Jaz screamed, as she walked over to him. "Put the gun down."

"Who the fuck is this nigga, and what the fuck just happened in here?" Devon asked, while pushing his way through, grabbing the stranger by the front of his jacket, and escorting him into the house.

Once he reached the living room, he observed how the Geechies worked quickly to tie Supreme down. Tape was quickly being wrapped around his wrists and ankles. Just as quickly, a gag was being placed over his mouth.

Supreme looked up from his awkward position to find Damion standing in the middle of his living room floor. He looked on with pleading eyes, hoping that Damion would put a stop to all of this. Supreme held his stare until something clicked inside of his mind. There was something familiar in the way Damion stared back at him. It was the same look he got from Devon the night he confronted him about his business.

"I knew it!" Supreme tried to say through the gag. "I'ma kill that bitch-ass nigga when I get my hands on him," Supreme mumbled.

"That's only if you come out of this alive, faggot!"

Toy was now standing beside Devon.

"Baby, please put the gun down. Let me take care of this," Jaz asked of him, as she replayed the scene of the day Devon had first arrived at her doorstep telling her that he had switched places with Damion.

After she found out all of the details to Devon's plan, she became desperate. So, she made a phone call—the call that she should have made years ago, but didn't find the need to until now.

The person at the other end of the phone line was more than happy to help out in Jaz's plan to prove her son's innocence. He would have done anything for her twins and why wouldn't he? He was their father.

For years, Mark Perez stood on the sidelines and watched his sons grow into incredible young men. With much pride, he observed their years of youth from the shadows. He was there always on those special occasions, graduations from elementary school then junior high school. He even sat at the back of the auditorium when Damion graduated from high school. He watched them from the bleachers when the boys played ball in the neighborhood parks. He also watched as the system stripped his youngest son Devon of his freedom, leaving Damion heartbroken from the separation.

So, when he received the phone call from Jaz, he was more than willing to help his son. He was willing to take the chance and even die for him if need be. Now was Mark's chance to be their father.

"Devon, baby, please, you have to put the gun down."

"No! Who the fuck is this?" Devon questioned Jaz, as he tossed Mark back and forth.

Jaz could see that Devon was not going to let up until she answered him. She never wanted her son to find out like this. Basically, she had no choice. She had to tell him the truth.

"Devon," Jaz slowly said, while closing her eyes, "this is your father."

Jaz always wondered what her sons would say if she had given them the chance to know the truth. She now regretted hiding all the facts. Her selfish need to protect them had stood in the way. She hadn't wanted Mark to be a part of their lives.

Sexy

"My father! What the fuck is this, a family reunion or a showdown?"

Everyone looked at Devon except Toy, who was only worried about his own ass. If they didn't get the information they had come for, he was a dead man.

Chapter 24

Days turned into nights and nights into days, while Damion continued to take his brother's place in a life he chose to never call his own. Time was running out. In a few days, Damion would be back on the streets where he belonged. Everything he had endured in the past few days would change his life forever. He would not be walking out of prison the same way that he walked in. Mentally, that is. This little experience was capable of straightening out most of the brothers who strolled into the prison system. Hopefully, his brother would be a better man because of it. For that, he would be grateful.

Devon had lived a life of destruction. Hustling was never supposed to be a glamorous business, but it became one. It was mainly for those who sought an outlet, an escape from the hood. Devon never got the concept, though, so he continued hustling, letting greed take over.

This is why he was so impressed with Marcus. He had taken a step forward in changing his future. He enrolled in a G.E.D. class, and participated in a few tutoring sessions with a teacher's aide. Whoever said that convicts couldn't be rehabilitated was wrong. Society always looked down on someone who served a prison sentence. It didn't matter how or why they were convicted. The reason why just didn't matter to those who ran the big corporations.

Well, in Damion's opinion, society was in for a big surprise. Damion and Marcus met at least twice a day in the library, where they both found peace of mind away from the other convicts and prison guards. With Daija's help, Marcus was able to get all of the materials he needed to gain his equivalency diploma.

"So what do you think, Dey? You think I'm ready for this test?" Marcus asked, while Damion looked over his work.

"You're more than ready. What I want to know is why you waited so long?"

"I never really thought about it. I was doing exactly what I knew how to do to survive." Marcus sighed, then continued. "Let me be straight up with you. Dey, at the time, school was corny to me. Getting an education was the last thing on my mind. I used to laugh at the niggas who carried their knapsacks around like a bunch of squares. Sometimes, after a good laugh, I would rob them of their lunch money. At the time, that seemed like much more fun."

"It seemed like fun, Marcus," Damion said, correcting Marcus on his grammar.

"Yeah, yeah, you know what I mean."

"Yeah, I know."

"Anyway, I guess I blamed them for my own inadequacy."

"Damn, bro, you using big words and shit. What's up with that?"

"Well, it's like you said, once I change my vocabulary, I can speak with a little degree of class. It will open up doors to a whole new world for me."

"You sure said that right. Okay, let's stop bullshittin' and get busy. The test is in two days."

Damion had to laugh at how easy it was for Marcus to go back and forth with his lingo. He was one of the few that were going to make it. On that, Damion would bet his life.

Later on in the day, Damion was scheduled to attend a rehab group by the name of A.S.A.T. According to the info he received from the other inmates, Devon's name had reached the top of the list. It was his turn to receive group therapy because Devon's crime was committed in Club Ecstasy where liquor was being served. He had to attend a drug program along with A.R.T. and Down on Violence.

Upon entering the room, the atmosphere held a sense of disapproval. No one wanted to be there. Damion took his place in line. First thing he needed to do was sign the contract, a contract that would hold Devon hostage for six months. If everything went well on the outside, Devon wouldn't be here to complete the program. They will both be on the streets. Nothing would be sweeter. Damion had to admit that he was horrified at the thought of having to discuss his or his brother's issues in front of a bunch of strangers.

He reached the front of the line, grabbed the necessary forms, and began to read the 101 rules on how to successfully complete the mandated program. He read on, and then discovered that A.S.A.T. was mainly for drug-addicted people who couldn't deal with the day-to-day pressures of life.

Damion continued to read down the line. There, at the far end of the page, he had to place his signature. Routinely, he was supposed to sign and begin the first session; however, he couldn't. Something was really bothering him about the contract. Devon was not a drug user. Frustrated with what he had in his hand, he walked over to where the counselors sat.

"Excuse me, but I can't sign this contract."

"And why is that, son?" Mr. Hill asked Damion.

Mr. Hill was a black brother in his mid-40s, who, at first sight, spoke a thousand words without even opening his mouth. You could just tell that Mr. Hill had personal and emotional experience in the drug life. Educational experience was later encountered in his groups.

"Because I'm not a drug user. This program is for people who have a drug problem," Damion replied, while passing the contract off.

"What's your name, son?"

Mr. Hill had experienced this type of attitude many times before. Denial was one of the biggest factors in recovery. Therefore, he was always ready to explain the true essence of the program he had grown to live by.

Damion refused to answer Mr. Hill's question. What was the point in him knowing Damion's name if he wasn't going to be a part of his groups?

"Okay, I'll tell you what. Let me take care of the others first. Then you and I can take a walk and talk about it."

"Talk about what? I already told you I don't use drugs."

"I heard you the first time. Be easy. You can make your decision after we talk."

Damion moved over to the side, allowing Mr. Hill to join the other guys who were more than thrilled to sign the contract. He observed how they unfolded chairs, forming a circle around the crowded room. As everyone began to take their places, another counselor stood up and began her speech.

"Good afternoon. My name is Mrs. Negron. I would like to welcome you to A.S.A.T., which stands for Alcohol and Substance Abuse Treatment program. We will begin by going around the room and introducing ourselves."

Damion had zoned out at this point. The negative energy he felt was not so much his refusal to do this program. It was deeper than that. He could feel his brother's energy running through him. Devon was on stress mode, and Damion could feel it. Before Damion could touch base with his brother mentally, Mr. Hill approached him from behind. Damion heard Mrs. Negron from a far distance talking to the group of men who sat in the circle. She was letting them know that it was their responsibility to be honest and open, that their participation and contribution to the group would allow the others to do the same.

"What's up?" Mr. Hill asked, as he tapped Damion on his shoulder. "Are you all right?"

Before he could respond, Mr. Hill placed his arm around Damion's shoulder and led him out into the hallway.

"Yeah, I'm good." Damion shoved Mr. Hill's arm away.

"Yo, chill, Mr. Aviles. I didn't mean any harm."

Damion felt stupid. He didn't usually behave so rudely. It was his surroundings that had him on edge.

"You don't seem all right. You got stress lines all over your forehead. Why don't you tell me what's going on, then we can talk about this contract."

Mr. Hill waved the document in front of his face.

"I already told you. I don't use drugs, and I don't feel this is the right program for me. I need to be in something that deals with money addiction."

Damion's tone was becoming arrogant. He was defensive and he wanted to make his point clear. That's it and that's all.

"All right, so you don't use drugs. Then why are you here?"

"What do you mean, why am I here?"

"Yeah, why are you here in prison?"

"Oh, I was convicted on a murder one charge."

"That's it?"

"Yeah, that's it. Why, was there supposed to be something else?"

"Let me ask you a question." Mr. Hill ignored Damion's question by asking one of his own. "What were you doing at the time when this crime was committed?"

"I was attending my aunt's wedding."

"No, son. What were you doing for a living?"

Damion had to think about that one. The brother was trying to make his point now.

"Behind the murder conviction was a life of what?" Hill continued on.

Pretending to be Devon was becoming difficult. He had to constantly remind himself that he was living a life that was not his own.

"I was hustling."

"Drugs?"

"Yeah."

"And you think that this program wouldn't benefit you because you didn't use your own product, right?"

"Well, no, I didn't say it wouldn't benefit me."

"Let me tell you a little story, Mr. Aviles, about how this works. The system, what we call the administration, is failing us. Programs that are very much needed to rehabilitate are being snatched away from under us every single day. The taxpayers believe that you guys already have too much. They have done away with the college courses, money addiction meetings, and some of the vocational programs. God knows what else they're going to snatch away from you all.

"I have made it my duty to educate our brothers by letting them know that they have choices in life. The streets have led them to the P-Nile, and the P-Nile will lead them back out. It's up to the brothers who enter to exit with something useful under their belts. Something that they could use to maintain a successful future with skills that maybe they can pass on to their sons."

Damion was now listening and became open-minded to what Hill had to say.

"If you were to decide to sign this contract and join us in our mission, then I have done my job. You may not have used drugs, Mr. Aviles, but you sure as hell played a major part. Your addiction is far worse than that of a drug addict."

"Why is that?" Damion asked, knowing the answer would be interesting.

"Because you did what you did for self-gain. You knew what you were doing out there. Your mind was clear. The addict used nine times out of ten out of ignorance, in order to feel good or suppress a feeling that they couldn't deal with at the time, losing themselves eventually to the streets. You sold that garbage to your own people to gain financial power."

With that said, Mr. Hill took in a deep breath, and held out the contract for Damion to sign.

After signing on the dotted line, Damion sat among his peers, listening to his brothers as they expressed in depth how they wanted to change. As each word was spoken, Damion sighed. And with each tear they cried, Damion realized that he had some issues of his own he needed to deal with.

Sexy

Chapter 25

Supreme struggled against the bandage that cut into his mouth deeply. He cursed the day he ever met Devon, his worst fucking nightmare. Devon was supposed to be his right-hand man, his boy, his friend. Supreme had taken him under his wing, schooled him on everything he needed to know about the drug game, and how did the motherfucker repay him? He stepped out of line when he went out on his own, taking a lot of Supreme's clientele with him.

Supreme had gotten word from one of his soldiers that Devon had plans to kill him and then take over all of what Supreme had built—his enterprise. This is the reason why Supreme had placed the hit on Devon's head. He would have never tried to hurt Devon if it wasn't for the shit that was going around. News of Devon's betrayal had hurt him far more than he led on. He was the brother he never had. The only person Supreme grew to trust. When the first hit wasn't successful, he placed another one.

Supreme had heard through the grapevine that Devon was fighting his case. Therefore, he had to make sure Devon never hit the street. If he had been released because of some technicality, Supreme would never have had a moment's rest. Fear of what Devon was capable of doing to him was cause for him to blow shit out of proportion. If Devon was anything like he used to be, Supreme was not coming out of any altercations regarding Devon alive.

But why involve his mom and her people? It was odd that they would get involved in a murder charge. *They're old school. This doesn't make sense,* Supreme quietly thought to himself as he watched the family reunion. Quickly, his eyes moved from side to side. Everyone was still.

In their same positions, they waited for the next move. Venus, however, wouldn't be a part of the second phase. She was too hysterical to even think straight. It was a shame, too, because Supreme had been ready to hit the pussy up. He looked down at his loyal companion. Blood was flowing from his partner's chest and back. Tears formed. The anger of being violated was a bit too much to handle. He was used to having everything under control.

Devon stared at Mark as his mother tried to give an explanation. Never in a million years did he ever think that his mother would've lied to him. The three of them, Jaz, Damion, and Devon, were supposed to be tighter than tight. Now, he wasn't sure about that anymore. Devon could hear his mother's voice, but he wasn't listening to a fucking thing she was saying.

For years, his brother and he longed to have a male figure in their lives. Yeah, they had Toni, Lizard, and Chase, but it wasn't the same as having a father. Late-night talks between the twins were always about the many questions they would ask if he showed up one day.

Whatever happened to her rules of taking care of each other? Of always protecting one another? Who was she protecting all of this time? Devon looked at Jaz with pain in his eyes.

Jaz saw the pain and bitterness behind his soft eyes, and felt like shit. She had always admired her son's strength. He was the warrior of the two. The strength was now gone. All she saw was pain and hatred. This situation was going to be difficult enough for her to explain. Unfortunately, now was not the time. They had come to get some information, and Jaz was determined not to leave without it.

Sadly, she had no regrets. She had to do what she had to do to keep Mark away from her boys. It was the only thing she could have done at the time.

Jaz turned her back on the both of them, and walked with her pistol in hand to where the Geechies surrounded Supreme. Jaz reached her hand forward, pulling the tape away from Supreme's mouth.

"Ouch, bitch!" Supreme lowered his head in hopes of getting some relief.

"I got your bitch, motherfucker," Jaz stated in a low tone, as she smacked Supreme across the face. "I'm the only one that's going to be talking around here. So, shut the fuck up and listen. Believe me; your life depends on it."

The Geechies were now moving in closer. The reason? To scare Supreme into giving Jaz the info they needed. They needed him to say in his own words how he had put a hit out on Devon's life and how Devon had killed in self-defense. They were all very much aware that Devon wouldn't get off completely; however, his sentence of twenty-five to life would be possibly modified once they presented the new evidence. Miracles do happen. That's what Jaz was striving for—a miracle.

"Supreme, I am going to be your worst nightmare if you don't give me what I came for."

Mark dug into his pocket and pulled out a mini-recorder. He brushed past Devon, saying, "Son, there is nothing I can say that will change the past. But, believe me, after today, prison will be only a memory."

Mark continued towards Jaz, content in knowing that he had a chance to help his son.

"Thank you," Jaz said, as she grabbed the recorder out of Mark's hand. She pressed the record button and shoved it into Supreme's face.

"Now, tell me again how you set Devon Aviles up."

Jaz pushed the recorder roughly into Supreme's mouth.

"I don't know what the fuck you're talkin' about, and get that shit out of my fuckin' face."

Right after that statement, Jaz rewound the tape, erasing what was just recorded, then shoved the metal instrument back into his face. Before she pressed the button, Jaz said one last time, "Sup, I advise you to do what you have to do to save your ass. You already destroyed my son's life. Please don't make me destroy yours."

Supreme sensed a little guilt creeping up on him. Things had really gotten out of hand. Supreme felt that if from the very beginning Devon would have showed his loyalty, none of this would have happened. Many times, Supreme reminisced on how close they once used to be.

"Listen, asshole, stop wasting my motherfuckin' time and tell it before I bash your head in," Tima, the youngest and still the spunkiest of the crew, screamed into Supreme's grill.

Because of her age, the twins were more like brothers to Tima. She stepped up, despite all of her efforts to keep cool, and cracked Supreme over the head with her .357 Magnum. Instantly, blood trickled down the side of Supreme's face. The agonizing moans could be heard throughout the house.

Venus watched from the corner of the room at how Damion's mother tormented Supreme. She wanted to get the fuck out of there, but couldn't move. Her legs were numb. Devon also stood in shock at how Tima was capable of inflicting pain on another human being. He had never seen that side of her, and now that he did, he didn't like it. He could sense her anger. The hurt of having to resort back to her old ways showed right through her.

Devon could also see that it didn't matter to any of them. They were all there giving up their lives for him. He never really understood the Geechies' relationship. He always figured that the Geechies were just all close friends, but it was much deeper than that. They would die for each other, no matter what the circumstances.

Mark had to play his part to the "T" in order for the plan to work. From his duffle bag he had stashed in the foyer, he pulled a sealed plastic huffy bag that contained a white substance. Thanks to his partner, he was able to enter the evidence room at the precinct and borrow a kilo of heroin. Mark placed the substance on top of a glass table that sat smack in the middle of Supreme's living room.

Jaz looked at the substance and then at Mark as though he was crazy.

"Mark, did you lose your goddamn mind?"

"No, why? If you're going to get him to talk, you have to threaten him with prison time, not bodily harm. Supreme isn't going to break down with a few blows to the head. But, if you threaten his freedom, the nigga will sing like a bird. You can relate to that, can't you?"

Jaz stared at him with daggers in her eyes.

"Now is not the time for your bullshit, Mark. I should have never asked your ignorant ass to help my son."

Jaz now forgot all about Supreme as she confronted Mark face-to-face.

"He's my son, too, Jaz. You're the one who decided to keep me away from them." Mark was not backing down.

Devon ran from where Mark had left him standing earlier and stood between them. He grabbed Mark by his collarbone, pushing him away from Jaz's face.

Satisfied that Mark didn't resist, he slowly and gently said, "If you ever disrespect my mom again, I will kill you!"

The heat that came out of Devon's mouth was sure to make any man squirm, but not Mark. He stood his ground, and then turned around to handle his business.

"You, Supreme, you know that I would love to send your ass up north for at least fifteen years, right? You must be aware of the Rock."

Supreme held a blank stare.

"If you don't, let me break it down for you." Mark circled Supreme several times while educating him on the drug laws. "It's the law that convicts drug offenders to years of imprisonment. Your time is due. So, you better think about it."

Through the living room window, Twista watched how Supreme had failed to protect himself. His loyalty for Supreme had vanished. So many times, Supreme treated him like a stepchild, ordering him around like a sucker, as though the world belonged to him. Yeah, Supreme was the boss, but to outright disrespect Twista was uncalled for. He had done it on a daily basis, and Twista was tired of his shit.

The trouble with Supreme was that he had allowed his lifestyle to go to his head. The power, money, and broads twisted his mind. Twista was not for sale anymore. He could no longer be bought by the luxuries Supreme had bestowed upon him. Twista had saved enough money to disappear. Although similar in many ways to Supreme, there was one slight difference; he had enough sense to walk away. Twista felt nothing as he walked down the alley and jumped into a cab.

"Where to, sir?"

"To the airport."

Twista leaned back in his seat and wished Supreme well. Supreme was the one who had always said a nigga had to be loyal to himself first before he could be loyal to anyone else. Well, those words that he preached so well had come back to bite him on the ass.

Chapter 26

After work, Brenda rushed home to prepare a home-cooked meal. She stopped by the grocery store, bought a few items, and then stopped by the liquor store to pick up a bottle of Chardonnay. While the music played in the background, Brenda popped the steaks in the oven, placed the shrimps on the steamer, then placed ice cubes in a silver bucket where the wine would sit for a while chilling. Brenda and Venus had made plans earlier in the week to eat a nice dinner and drink a little something light before they hit the club for a ladies' night out.

Thanks to the delivery guy who showed up early, Brenda had been able to get her hands on their gear for the evening. Gucci's new fall collection was off the hook. She couldn't resist stashing a few garments into her bag before leaving for the day.

She was really looking forward to a night out. The store had been hectic all week with their annual clearance sale going on. Brenda was beat. Not only was she going to look fly thanks to Gucci, she had also gotten paid, so her pockets were looking sweet. Everything was all set to go. There was one problem, though. Venus was nowhere to be found.

According to Venus's new boss, Demonic, Venus had left her job early and was not expected back until Monday. They usually touched base throughout the day; however, today was different. Brenda had not heard anything, not a word from Venus. She was becoming increasingly worried by the moment. Brenda dialed Venus's celly once again, this time leaving a message on her voicemail.

"Hey, girl, what's up with you? Please call me. I am getting worried. I thought we had plans to go out tonight?"

* * * * *

Meanwhile, back at Supreme's place, Venus was still huddled in a corner. She felt her cell phone vibrate several times. She knew that it had to be Brenda, because the only other person who had her number was standing right in front of her. Trying to ignore the phone, Venus started concentrating on the man who stood in the middle of the living room floor, Damion. There was something different about him: his voice, his walk, his movements, and the way he popped his neck whenever he spoke. Everything about him was out of the norm.

She listened to Jaz and Mark discussing their sons as though there was no one else in the room, arguing and fussing about who was responsible for this or that. Damion had mentioned to her briefly that his twin brother was doing time at Sing-Sing. He never really got into details about his parents, though. You didn't have to be a genius to know that something was not right in their family.

Venus had built up enough strength to confront the situation. There were no more tears or fear of what stood before her. She only felt anger and confusion towards all the bullshit she was listening to. Now, she was the one who

188

wanted answers. That's what she had come for, and that's what she was going to get.

Venus was not going to tolerate any more games from Damion or his psycho friends. She wasn't about to go down with him for a body. Venus had just begun to live her life, and she had too many things yet to do. She had been released from prison a few days ago and already she was caught up in some nigga's shit—shit that could cause her a violation or, worse, a whole new number.

Venus was playing the tape back as she started to lift herself from her current position. Scenes of Bedford Hills kept popping into her mind. She had allowed her emotions for Damion to get the best of her. Venus knew better. All she wanted was a good man who she could bond with, love, and be strong with. What she had found was a man whom she diagnosed as a schizophrenic.

Venus glanced around the room for a way out. She watched as the Geechies, Jaz, and now Damion inflicted pain on Supreme, causing him to scream in agony. The diabolic look on their faces was enough to make a nigga commit suicide. She had decided at that moment that she was not ready to die. Venus adjusted her borrowed mink, ran her fingers through her hair, hoping to put it back in its place, and then walked towards the center of the room.

Devon noticed when Venus began to move. The look of craze on her face made him question her intentions. As she slowly glided in his direction, he realized he had made a big mistake by bringing her along. She didn't look right. Her troubled eyes and empty look made him feel nothing but sympathy for her. Unfortunately, she didn't feel the same about him.

Quickly, before Devon was able to move aside, Venus lifted her hand and smacked the shit out of him. Everyone turned around in his direction at the sound of flesh connecting.

"What the fuck?" is all he could say, as he reached out and grabbed her wrist.

Devon pushed Venus hard enough for her to fall flat on her ass, but she didn't. Her movements were structured and organized. Venus grabbed the .22 caliber pistol she had strapped to her thigh.

While pointing the weapon at Devon's face, she screamed uncontrollably, "You no good motherfucker, how can you put me in such a fucked-up position? You know I can't afford to be caught up in no fuckin' kidnapping or murder! I thought you were fuckin' different! You're just like all the other motherfuckers I've come across that hide behind a fuckin' suit!"

Venus was now fuming from her mouth. She was really losing it. So much so that she didn't notice Tima standing behind her, pointing her Glock straight at her skull.

"Venus, listen." Devon raised his hands in a "be easy" gesture.

"Don't say shit, you selfish piece of shit! Now, let him go, Damion!" Venus pointed at Supreme with her free hand.

Devon could not believe this shit. It was just his fucking luck. He had no idea what he was going to say next to convince Venus that this is what needed to be done in order to get a confession out of Supreme. Jaz came at Venus strongly and stood directly in front of Devon, facing Venus head on.

"Put the fuckin' gun down."

Noticing that her son was stuck, Jaz had to intervene. Venus's action was so unexpected. Jaz sympathized with Venus, but she was not going to allow her dramatic ass to blow their whole operation. Venus challenging Devon was out of the question.

"Put the fuckin' gun down. I'm not going to ask you again."

Jaz moved forward, and Tima moved in, too.

"I'm giving you two seconds or you're going to be the one laid out on this floor."

Venus knew better than to deceive Jaz, who was a woman of her word. But she didn't give a fuck. Venus was in too deep. As far as she was concerned, this shit wasn't going down like this. Not if she could help it.

"I ain't putting shit down. Do you have any idea what the fuck you guys are doing? Are you fuckin' crazy, Jaz?"

Venus was now shaking as she waited for Jaz to respond.

"Yeah, I do. Yes, I am. And, yes, you're going to put that piece of shit metal down. Now give me the fuckin' gun. I don't have time to explain any of this to you right now, Venus. You're going to have to trust me. Put the gun down before you hurt someone."

Backing away from Jaz, Venus walked right into the steel revolver Tima was so eager to fire.

"Bitch, put the fuckin' gun down now. This is your last warning," Tima yelled into Venus's ear. "This is why you don't bring extra baggage when we do shit." Tima's statement was directed to Jaz.

Things were getting crazier by the second. Venus's emotions were uncontrollable. They needed Supreme to talk, that's it.

Just then, Mark opened up his leather bomber. There hanging on his neck was a silver chain. As Venus looked on, she saw that he was wearing a badge that hung low to the middle of his chest.

"Oh, shit," Venus said, not believing her eyes. *These people even have the po-po down with this shit,* she thought.

As Venus lowered her gun, she said to anyone that was within earshot, "This shit is unbelievable. You motherfuckers are going down."

Now, totally defeated by everyone in the room, Venus lowered herself on to the nearest chair.

"Why are you all doing this crazy-ass shit? I thought this was going to be something easy. Come in, get the info, and then get out."

Devon stopped in front of her. "Listen, Vee, I know what you must be thinking, but believe me, I am still the man who took you out on your first date. I am still the man who bumped into you on 125th Street."

While Venus was trying to be a hero, Devon had to come up with a way of getting Venus to calm down. What better way than to act like the man she had fallen in love with—his brother? It was like the movie, the women with two faces. Damion was the soft, sensitive type, and Devon's hardcore style wouldn't work at that present moment.

"Baby, please, you need to calm down. I need you to focus on what we came here to do." Devon was now holding Venus's hand.

"Dey, why? Why the fuck are you getting yourself caught up in this type of madness? Why the fuck are you acting like I'm supposed to be okay with all of this shit?"

"Because I have to. My brother is locked up for protecting me. I owe it to him."

As they were having their moment, Supreme was squirming in his seat, trying to release himself. He was talking loudly from underneath the bondage that Jaz had to replace.

"What the hell is wrong with you?" Venus questioned him boldly.

Supreme's eyes moved from Devon to Venus. He was trying to tell them something. Mainly it was for her. He was trying to tell her not to fall for Devon's line. He was not Damion, but Devon. Anybody who knew the twins could tell the difference between them. It was obvious to him that Venus didn't know one from the other. Supreme had to warn her. She was the weakest link. She was the one that would fall short. If he could just get her to take the bondage off, he could blow up Devon's spot.

Chapter 27

Toy had suspected that things weren't going to go down the way that Devon had planned. One could never be too sure in the game. So, two days prior, he had connected with two of his boys, Jack and Brooklyn. He was unable to find Scoop, but left word that his services were very much needed.

During his meeting with Jack and Brooklyn, Scoop showed up scheming, quick to demonstrate his loyalty to the family who had provided him with the same. Living and growing up in different parts of the city, they found that they only had one thing in common— their devotion to the family and to each other. While incarcerated up north, they vowed that no matter where life's course would take them, they would abandon everything at a drop of a hat, if ever needed. Toy knew that he could depend on them.

Because of his backstabbing ways, mainly his betrayal toward Supreme, Toy needed a backup plan. Toy fell back while Devon, who he still thought was Damion, Venus, Jaz, and the Geechies played out their superhero roles. He had to admit that their efforts stood to be rewarded if they had been up for the Academy Awards. However, he could see that despite all their efforts they were never going to get Supreme to talk. They showed their weaknesses at every turn.

Reassured that his way would be much more effective, Toy walked over to where Supreme was still strapped and gagged. His squirming was getting to be real pathetic. Supreme's pleads was a sucker's cry for a nigga who thought he owned the streets, let alone the world. Where were his balls now?

"Shut the fuck up, Sup!" Toy hollered, while striking Supreme on the back of his head.

Toy's lack of patience caused him to become frustrated with the whole scenario. He wanted to take matters into his own hands. The scene that played out in his mind was one of the many that he had envisioned for Supreme. A smile came to his lips as he thought about how sooner than later that scene would become a reality.

Jack, Brooklyn, and Scoop waited outside the brownstone with their backs leaning up against the cold brick walls. The atmosphere was exactly how they wanted it to be, calm and quiet. Rush hour had finally died down. Everyone who lived on the block was now tucked away in their domains. With no interference from nosey neighbors, they would be able to go in, grab the target, and escape without anyone knowing what was going on around them.

They began to adjust their gear, making mental calculations of the crime they were about to play out. Scoop, the youngest and the most eager, was more than willing to run up in Supreme's crib and blow shit the fuck up. Brooklyn, who got his way all the way, enjoyed putting pressure on niggas who thought they were road dawgs. Jack was the laid-back one of the three; observation was the key to his success. Going down for the cause was easy for him. But, he was the thinker, the one who outlined all of their operations.

All dressed in black-hooded jackets, baggy jeans, and custom-made Timbs, they appeared to be just three thugs getting ready to commit a robbery. If only it was that simple.

Toy had supplied them with masks, but they refused to wear them. They enjoyed knowing that their naked faces would be the last ones their victim would see. The thrill of the victim looking head-on made their dicks hard. For them, it was better than getting a raw piece of ass at the end of the day.

Jack looked at his watch, a gift from his lady, and gave them a few more seconds to gather up their nerves. Five...four...three...two...one.

"Go!" Jack whispered.

Quickly finding the power box, Brooklyn pulled on all of the wires, causing the brownstone to go completely dark. They dashed through the main floor, passing the kitchen and dining room, and entering straight into the parlor. Scoop crept around the room in search of Supreme, while Jack pointed his miniature flashlight in different directions. Brooklyn crawled on the floor, grabbing the first group by the ankles. One by one, they fell. Devastated by the sudden attack, none of them dared to use their weapons for fear of shooting each other.

Getting in and out would be easier than what they thought. With target in hand, they were going to get out of the brownstone and onto the street without anyone reacting.

"Damn, nigga, just walk," Brooklyn told Supreme, as he pushed him towards the van they had stolen a few hours earlier.

Supreme was struggling against their grip. He refused to go down without a fight. Finally, after a few seconds of trying to get Supreme into the van, Scoop pistol-whipped him, knocking Supreme the fuck out.

Jack jumped into the driver's seat, as Brooklyn and Scoop threw Supreme in, jumped in themselves, and slammed the doors. Some things were unavoidable. Jack hoped that Scoop hadn't caused permanent damage.

Racing through the FDR Drive and onto the Deegan Expressway heading north, Jack, Brooklyn, and Scoop sat quietly contemplating their next move. But, first, they needed to get to their destination.

Chapter 28

The choices Devon had made throughout his lifetime weren't always the right ones. Surely there were consequences behind everything he chose to do, but what he was experiencing at this very moment was ridiculous. Nothing else could have possibly gone wrong. Something that was supposed to be so simple was turning out to be the most difficult thing for them all.

Time was running out and he had yet to get the information he needed. Devon thought about how he had let Damion down and everyone else who was involved. His people had gone out on a limb for him, and what did he give them back in return—zero. This was a hard pill to swallow.

Devon adjusted his eyes and was now able to see shadows dancing off the cream-colored walls. One by one, they all began to get up from their awkward positions. No one dared to speak, though. They didn't know for sure if there was still someone else in the room. Toy knew, though, that his partners were long gone and that nothing else would happen. Devon, on the other hand, was grateful that no one was hurt. Toy stood in front of Devon and reached out his hand. He helped him get on his feet, and then began to shout out orders.

"They're gone, you guys. You can switch the lights back on. We need to see what the fuck just went down."

"What the fuck do you think went down?" Devon hollered.

"Whoever those niggas were they just took off with Supreme," Tima said, as she tried to brush off the shock of it all, and then ran to the windows.

"You are a real dumb ass. Get the fuck away from that window, girl," Toy screamed at Tima.

"Who the fuck are you calling a dumb ass, you chump-ass bitch?" Tima changed course as soon as she heard the way that Toy was talking to her. All up in his face now, Tima punched him so hard that his nose began to bleed.

"Yo, you's about a dumb bit...!"

Before Toy was able to say the "B" word, Devon grabbed him by the arm.

"Yo, chill, man, we ain't got no time for this. We need to figure out what the fuck is going on," Devon said, then walked away.

"This shit was supposed to be on the hush-hush, and I know that my people wouldn't dare go outside of our crew to speak to no one. So, I figure it could only be you and yours," Trouble said, as she stepped up and pointed straight at Toy's face. "One of you motherfuckers just played yourself," Trouble continued on, as everyone else just watched her in action.

"Well, it wasn't me. I didn't even know you psychos were going to do something so stupid. And another thing, what is it this so-called Supreme has on you that you are trying to get?" Venus asked, directing the question at Devon.

"None of your business," Devon shot back.

"None of my business, you no-good, mixed-breed motherfucker?"

Venus wasn't referring to his culture or heritage. She was more on the lines of him being half-human and half-animal.

"Okay, okay, chill. We are not going to get anywhere by fighting each other. We need to stick together to figure this shit out." Jaz had had just about enough of the bullshit.

"First of all, we need to get the fuck out of here," Mark responded to Jaz's aggravation.

"You're right. Let's get the hell out of here."

Again, Jaz was the one leading the way. Nothing much had changed when it came to the Geechies. They always waited for Jaz or Trouble to make the last call. Together, they left Supreme's crib. Not the same way that they came in, though. They left through the front door, a day late and a dollar short.

With all of the disappointments Devon had endured throughout the last four years, he honestly believed that this fucked-up situation would one day come to an end. He wasn't about to give up on his quest for the truth.

Turning towards Toy as they reached the street, Devon asked, "Okay, nigga, where he at?"

"What? You act like I had something to do with his sudden departure." Toy's slick grin gave him away.

"You did. You think I don't know how trifling your ass can be?"

"Trifling? Nigga, please. I was only trying to help your dumb ass. Your plan got all fucked up thanks to your people." Toy let the cat out of the bag. He continued to talk until he noticed Devon's smile. "What the fuck are you smiling about, Dey?"

"You. Now tell me what you did with him."

"All right. I had my boys take him someplace where we're sure to make him talk."

"Where?" Devon was practically running down the street towards his ride.

"Chill, Dey. Where the fuck are you going?" Toy asked between breaths.

Devon stopped abruptly, grabbed Toy by his throat, and threw his ass up against some steel gates.

"What the fuck you mean where I'm going? We're going to get Supreme and get the fuckin' info I need in order to one, get my brother out of jail, and two, murder his sorry ass."

Devon's breath was hot on Toy's face. Toy didn't want to cross Devon or say anything that would set him off, so he nodded his head in agreement. Devon was already enraged, so much so that Toy began to question himself. He hoped that he had done the right thing.

Venus walked out of the brownstone alone. Everyone else had gone their separate ways, including Damion. She was hurt. Not once did he look back at her as he ran down the street with Toy. Venus had no understanding as to what was really going on. Basically, she was at a point that she didn't want to know either. Her investigating days were over. All she wanted was to forget that any of this had happened. Go home, jump into a nice warm bath, maybe have a little of that wine she knew Brenda had on ice. It was déjà vu. She had seen herself doing exactly the same thing that she was doing now. Maybe it was in her dreams.

Suddenly, the celly vibrated. Without looking at it, she answered.

"Hello."

"Girl, where have you been? I've been so worried about you."

"It's a long story," Venus said, as tears welled up in her eyes.

"Well, you better start talking."

"Not right now, Bee. I'm on my way home. I'll explain once I get there."

"All right, girl, hurry up. I won't rest until you are in this house."

Venus closed her phone, then thought about how close she and Brenda had become. It really meant a lot to her that she had someone who cared.

* * * * *

Jaz and Trouble paced back and forth while telling Toni everything that had happened.

"So what you're telling me is that you called Mr. Perez?"

"Yes, baby, I had to."

"You had to?" Toni stood up from her seat.

"Is that all you're thinking about, Toni? I needed him to help us. Baby, I didn't have a choice."

"You didn't have a choice? Oh, girl, you had a choice! You just chose the wrong one!"

"Please, Toni, you are getting all bent out of shape for nothing." Jaz reached out to touch her lover.

"Oh, you think it's for nothing, huh? Well, what was the fuckin' point in calling him then? Did you get the fuckin' information you needed to help our sons?"

"No," Jaz answered softly.

She knew where Toni was going. Toni was far from stupid.

"But you decided once again to do things on your own without telling me anything, right? All right, Jaz, let me give it to you like this."

Toni was the one who was now pacing, while Jaz sat down and Trouble stood there listening to the pain in Toni's voice.

"You decided to call the man who we tried to keep away from the boys. For years, you told them your own version of their father's existence, and now you have two problems. Now they are going to want answers. What are you going to say to them, Jaz? 'Oops, I ran into him at the fuckin' store?' Our sons are never going to believe in us again. Tell me, what the fuck are you going to say?"

Toni was more than hurt by Jaz's action. She felt betrayed. She had underestimated Jaz's love and respect for her.

"You know what? Don't even bother to answer that?"

Toni walked into their bedroom, and several minutes later, she walked out with a duffle bag slung over her shoulder.

"Where are you going, baby? Why are you buggin'?"

"Jaz, I'm not the one who is buggin'. I allowed you to deceive me once, and now you have done it again. Do you think I'm going to stand around and watch Perez play daddy? I don't think so. I'm out."

"Out! Where are you going, baby?" Jaz ran towards Toni. "Please, baby, don't do this."

"Nah, it's all right. I'm getting the fuck away from you before I hurt your sneaky ass."

Toni pushed Jaz out of the way, headed for the door, and walked out. Jaz was stuck. She wanted to go after her, but her legs wouldn't move. Deep down inside, she knew that she had fucked up. However, what Toni didn't understand was that when it came to her sons, there was no limit to what she would do. Calling Mark was the only thing she had thought of at the time. Desperate times called for desperate measures.

Chapter 29

Mail call was at six p.m. right after the count, and Damion hoped they would call his name, but for what? He wasn't sure. It wasn't like anyone knew he was in jail. The thought of it still excited him, though. It's sad how when a nigga got locked up it would only be a matter of time that he desired to hear from someone from the outside world.

That morning, Damion had tried to call the attorney he had hired to handle Devon's case. He was sure the judge had come to a decision by now. The waiting period was beyond nerve-wracking. Unfortunately, the attorney was not available to take his call. That's what his secretary had said anyway.

Not being able to connect with anyone made Damion feel isolated. Being in the dark was a fucked-up feeling. Marcus had tried to reassure him that everything would work out; however, for some reason, Damion felt differently. He could feel his brother's energy. Something had gone wrong.

He could also feel Venus. The separation was taking its toll. It made him realize that he had fallen in love with her. From the moment they met, there was an instant connection. She was exactly what he had been looking for in a woman. She was strong, witty, sexy, intelligent, dedicated, understanding, motivated, fascinating, loving, noble, responsible, and so much more. She fought her own battles and stood her ground. Her independence is what really captured him; her will to make it out in the free world without a handout. Damion admired her for her courage. She reminded him a lot of his mother. He had made a vow at that moment to let her know how special she really was to him.

Count time came and went, along with mail call. The day was almost over, and still he had no idea what the outcome was of Devon's plans. His days in prison were numbered. He couldn't wait to get out. It felt as though he really was the one sentenced to do time. Day after day, he fell back to observe how so many brothers had lost their lives to the struggle. He wanted to reach out to the few he had come across, but how could he? This wasn't his life. It might seem normal to the average nigga if they knew the truth.

Damion had tried to go with the flow within the prison walls. But, enough was enough. He wanted to get the fuck out of there. He wanted to go and tell his woman that he never wanted to be separated from her again.

It was a big possibility that she had figured out the truth by now. If not, he would have to tell her. Damion didn't want to start their relationship based on a bunch of lies. He had the heart of a man, a real man.

"Where the fuck are you, Devon?" Damion asked, as he laid back on his bunk.

* * * * *

Driving up north, Devon had finally reached the exit that would lead him back to Supreme. Looking down at his watch, he realized he had been on the road for more than an hour. Turning off onto a dirt road, Toy instructed him to follow the maze of trees. It was dark as hell. To make matters worse, it had started to rain. Devon found it extremely difficult to see anything in front of him. He slowed down and used his judgment, while cursing Toy out with every turn.

Toy sat there speechless, praying that once Devon, who he thought was Damion, saw exactly how he was going to get Supreme to confess, he would calm down. If not, then fuck it. Toy really didn't give a fuck either way. He had to do whatever it took to save his own ass. Getting rid of Devon would be an added bonus. Then he didn't have to deal with nobody's shit.

At the end of the road, Devon came to a complete halt. Directly in front of him was a small wooden structure. It stood about two-stories high with large windows. What looked to him like a small house was not. The rain had slowed down some, making the barn come into view.

It was a bit too quiet for his taste. He never was a country boy. Devon was used to the hustle of the city life. He turned off the ignition, climbed out of the car, and then circled over to the other side. Toy was already reaching for the door handle. Devon had replaced the clip in his gun and was ready to pop some holes in Toy, when he noticed that Toy swung the passenger's side door open.

"Get your ass out of the car."

"Chill, nigga. Why the fuck are you so hostile?"

"Just come on, man. You got me out here in hillbilly land."

Devon took Toy by the arm. He placed the gun on his temple and ordered him to move forward slowly.

"Why you trippin', son?"

"You must think I'm a real sucker. You think I don't know what your ass was thinking when you did this dumb shit?"

"I don't know what you're talking about, Dey. I was—"

"Shut the fuck up and just walk."

Before they entered the old, decrepit barn, Devon had checked the grounds. The place must have been abandoned for a very long time. He couldn't find anything that told him otherwise. There was nothing out of the ordinary, just an old van parked by the back door. Toy had tried to explain that it belonged to his homeboys who had kidnapped Supreme.

When Devon finally felt at ease, he entered the old barn. Toy called out before trying to take another step. He didn't want to get accidentally shot up. Jack, Brooklyn, and Scoop were always ready for some action. Jack...well, he usually would have stayed in the cut, allowing Brooklyn to take the lead. However, today, Jack was on the front line. He was like a mountain lion, observing his surroundings and then stepping out to do his thing, until he was sure that Toy and Devon weren't the enemies crossing the enemy line. He laid low.

Toy and Devon stood by the doorway until they were cleared by Jack, who had stepped out from behind the shadows.

"Come on, nigga. We ain't got all day." Jack motioned for them to follow.

Devon looked around skeptically. The wooden structure had been gutted out. It looked like some shit out of a Western flick. Somewhere in the back stalls that housed horses, Supreme had been tied up and gagged once again. He had been hanging in mid-air, attached to the old ceiling beams. The long chains that were wrapped around his wrists cut deep, causing blood to drip down his arms. The scene was a lot like the Crucifixion of Jesus Christ. The smell of urine and shit attacked Devon's nostrils before he was able to get up closer. "What the fuck!"

"Yeah, kid, I told you we wasn't playin' no motherfuckin' games," Toy hollered at Supreme.

"Yo, Toy, you are buggin'. You ain't trying to help my brother out. You are trying to make a nigga catch a new felony. You're trying to shut the lights off."

Devon's palms became cold, which was strange because his body was burning up. Sweat was starting to form beneath his hairline. He wiped the moisture with the sleeve of his coat. Thoughts of him being sentenced to death row jumped around in his head. Devon had to make Supreme talk, then discard of his remains. Toy's boys stood around Supreme, eager, waiting for Devon to get the full impact of what was about to go down.

In their hands, they held black, solid steel blackjacks, a complimentary gift from the 23rd Precinct. Slowly, Scoop lowered Supreme's body. The sound of the chairs created an echo throughout the empty room. Devon's conscience began to fuck with him. He couldn't move forward towards the dangling body. A big part of him wanted to tell these fools to release him. The other part, the man, the thug, the beast was about to be unleashed. He was no sucker. His ego was definitely getting in the way. The street life had really changed him. All of the disappointments from the game left no room for a soft heart.

Supreme knew his current situation was not going to have a happy ending. However, coming to grips with death was another story all together. He never dreamed that his final days, hours, and minutes would be spent being tortured. His life of a drug dealer was supposed to be temporary. He had become hooked on the rush, on the fact that he had power, money, and respect. The violence came after. Whenever he felt that he was about to lose his wealth, that's when his guns came into play, threatening anyone who tried to destroy what he had built.

The illusion that he was untouchable was beyond comprehension. What made him think for one minute that he was exempt to the violence or even death? None of this was new. It had all been done before. The Dons of Spanish Harlem never got the chance to shine, and if they did, it was only for a short time. Just enough time to make themselves street legends. If their streets could talk, they would have warned Supreme of the dangers that lay ahead. Now, with a million and one regrets, he stared into the eyes of the last man he had wanted to see, the man whom he had betrayed for the almighty dollar. There was no turning back now.

Devon is not about to undo what already has been done, Supreme thought, as the first blow connected.

Devon could hear the cracking of the bones. Blood was spraying freely. Devon watched as Brooklyn and Scoop swung into Supreme with full force. Supreme's body jerked forward as Brooklyn connected from behind, then backwards as Scoop connected from the front. They laughed as Supreme yelled in agony. Devon had to look away at times. He could feel the pain run through his own body. When he couldn't take the screams anymore, he told them to stop.

"Enough!" Devon ordered from where he stood.

Suddenly, all movement stopped. Only the sound of Supreme's moans could now be heard. His breathing was shallow, as he hung in the air with nowhere to go. Devon hoped that he wasn't unconscious, because then all of this would have been for nothing. He told Jack to release him. Although it was too late to turn the tables around, he didn't want another body added to his pedigree.

"Release him?" Jack questioned Devon.

"Yeah, release him."

"Come on, man. Shit just started getting good." Jack's smile twisted. He had been enjoying himself.

Brooklyn tossed his weapon, walked over to the wall, and detached the chain from where it was suspended.

Supreme's body dropped, motionless.

Chapter 30

Somewhere in the shuffle, Devon's legal mail was mixed up with some packages. So, instead of the legal mail arriving at the law library, the envelope sat among a bunch of UPS packages in the facility package room. Mr. Padilla, his attorney, had forwarded the judge's response as soon as he was through arguing Devon's appeal.

The Honorable Judge Ramirez had granted them a new trial. Upon arriving at his office located in the Woolworth Building on Broadway, Mr. Padilla grabbed all of his messages from his paralegal, walked into his office, and locked the door behind him. He threw his briefcase onto a glass table, placed all of his messages on his desk, and then sat down. Mr. Padilla leaned back and took several deep breaths. It had taken him years of research to get the decision he had received today. Because of the lack of self-defense laws in New York State, Mr. Padilla had to go down some other avenues. These avenues had produced many cases similar to Devon's, and these cases had been overturned at a second hearing. That's exactly what he had been striving for. Devon had received a raw deal. Now it was up to him to prove it.

Meanwhile, back at Sing-Sing, Damion was awakened by the sound of the officers' voices.

"Devon Aviles!"

Damion immediately jumped up from his bunk.

"Yeah, what's up?"

"You got a package. You need to get yourself together and go on the next movement."

"All right."

At the package room, Damion showed his ID card. The officer walked over to a shelf and brought back a large yellow envelope.

"There was a mix-up with the packages that were brought in today. This was supposed to go up to the law library," the C.O. explained, while handing it to Damion.

"Thanks. Good lookin'."

Damion was not expecting anything, especially not from Devon's attorney. Damion's hands began to shake as he held the envelope. He had been discouraged by Mr. Padilla's statement prior to the scheme Devon had concocted. Those discouraging words from Mr. Padilla stopped Damion from tearing into the contents.

Walking slowly back towards the cellblock, visions of Devon and him appeared. He thought about how good it would feel to be in the free world once again with his brother. All of the time that had passed them by hadn't caused a gap in their relationship, but he missed him. They could never make up for lost time. Never be able to capture those moments again. But, they sure as hell could make the rest of their time here on earth much more worthwhile. Damion knew that if his brother was granted a second chance at life, he would do the right thing, never again to return to the streets as a drug dealer.

Before reaching the block, Marcus came out of nowhere holding a piece of paper in his hand, punching the air as if shadowboxing.

"Yo, Dey, slow down, man." Marcus was now running towards him. "You are not going to believe this shit." Marcus placed the letter into Damion's hand. "Read it, man."

Damion read the heading and realized that the letter was sent from the Department of Education. Further down, he read all of the scores, and finally, at the bottom of the page, was Marcus's G.E.D. diploma. Marcus had passed the test. Pride read on Damion's face as he grabbed Marcus into a bear hug and embraced him.

"I told you, you could do it, nigga. I'm so fuckin' proud of you."

Tears formed in Damion's eyes. Marcus had worked hard to obtain this single document that would open new doors for him.

"We have to celebrate," Marcus said, as they pushed away from their brotherly embrace.

"Yeah, man. You should be real proud of yourself."

"Yo, what's that?"

The subject changed once Marcus glanced at the envelope in Damion's hand.

"It's something for Devon from his attorney."

"What?"

"I don't know. Probably ain't shit but bad news."

"How do you know, man? Open that shit up and let's find out."

"Nah, I'm just gonna chill and hold off until Devon comes back. Then he can open it himself."

"Oh hell no!" Marcus grabbed the envelope and began to tear it apart.

"Yo, chill, Mar." Damion tried to reach for it, but Marcus turned his back on him.

"Nah, nigga, you chill. Do you have any idea how long your brother has been waiting for something like this?"

Damion stood still. Marcus was right. How dare he think of himself at a moment like this? This wasn't about him. This was about Devon. He just didn't want any disappointments.

"Oh yeah, oh yeah!" Marcus sang, as he turned around and started dancing circles around Damion.

"What, nigga?"

From the look on Marcus's face, it was good news.

"Oh hell no! You didn't want to read it, remember?" Marcus replied, extending his arm over his head, teasing Damion.

"Stop playing, Mar, and give me the fuckin' letter."

Marcus let his arm down, then handed Damion the good news. Damion read the letter word for word. He could not believe what was there in black and white in big, bold letters: GRANTED.

Damion began to do a dance of his own. While chanting "Oh yeah, oh yeah," Damion walked quickly towards his block.

"Where are you going, Dey?" Marcus yelled down the hall.

"I got some phone calls to make. I'll catch up with you later," Damion said, as he disappeared.

Marcus looked down at his own success. Things were really looking up. Now, he believed that he could accomplish anything. His next move would be to find his sister Venus.

Chapter 31

Jaz couldn't stop crying. She prayed that the feelings she was going through would subside. The feeling of being a failure had to pass by as quickly as possible. There was no time to start feeling sorry for herself. Jaz had to figure out where in the hell her son had gone. She sat by the phone hoping that she would get word soon.

Jaz was so angry at Toni for walking out on her. Surely Toni had to know that she didn't mean to deceive her. How could she possibly blame her, when her back was against the wall? Granted, Jaz should have told her what she had planned, but it was too late for all that now. Toni had said it clearly before she walked out that Jaz had taken her for granted. Now that Jaz thought about it, it was true. Jaz needed Toni home. Devon had no idea how his decision to switch places with Damion had affected everyone who loved and cared about him. Their lives could be changed once again.

While Jaz wiped the tears from her eyes, she continuously pressed the redial button on her celly, leaving her home phone free for any incoming calls. All she got was Damion's voicemail. Devon had no idea what he was doing to her nerves. She slammed the phone down on her glass end table after her last attempt of reaching him.

"God, please, I'm begging you. Keep my son safe, Lord. Lord, can you please open a way for my son to contact me? My life would be meaningless if something happened to him. Amen."

Just as Jaz finished saying those last few words, her home phone began to ring. She stared at her caller ID. On the screen appeared the word "unavailable". She usually didn't accept these types of calls. However, the situation was different.

"Hello, who is this?" Jaz barked into the receiver.

"You have a collect call from Devon Aviles from Sing-Sing Correctional Facility," the automated machine announced. "If you would like to accept this call, please press 3." Before the automated voice completed the request, Jaz was already bawling into the phone.

"Mom...Mom, what's wrong? What happened? Mom!"

Jaz tried to control herself, but she couldn't. She was hyperventilating.

"Mom, calm down. What the fuck is going on over there?"

In between sobs, Jaz tried to tell Damion what a mess things had turned into. Damion couldn't understand a word of what she was trying to say. He allowed her to vent, cry, talk, cry some more, and scream until he couldn't stand the drama any longer.

"Ma, you have to fuckin' chill! I don't understand shit you're saying." Damion was on the edge of his seat with worry. All kind of negative shit was running through his mind. "Where's Devon?"

Several seconds had passed and Damion could tell that Jaz was coming to grips. So, he asked her again, "Where's Devon, Mom?"

"I don't know."

"What do you mean you don't know? What happened?"

"We had the whole thing planned out. We were supposed to go in, get the information from Supreme, and then get out."

"What went wrong?"

"Someone had other plans for him. While we were in the middle of doing our thing, the lights went out and they kidnapped Supreme."

"Kidnapped Supreme! You mean to tell me that someone other than the crew took his ass against his will?"

"Yeah. No one else knew what we were doing, so it had to be against his will."

"Mom, listen. I just received notice that Devon is going to get a new trial. With that information, it is possible that he can either be released or get a shorter sentence."

"Oh my God, Dey! What are we going to do?"

"I don't know. Let me think."

Damion sat still holding the phone close to his ear as he thought of a way to get in contact with his brother. Then the light bulb went off in his head.

"Ma, I just thought of something. Is Devon still using my ride?"

"Yes, I think so. Last time I checked, he was still using it."

"Okay, listen carefully. When I first purchased my ride, I joined an auto club. Part of the package deal was placing a small detector under the hood. The detector would be activated if ever I reported the car stolen."

"What's the name of this club, baby?"

"Double-A. Okay, now why don't you call?"

"Don't you think it would sound better coming from you?"

"How am I supposed to call?"

"Hold on." Jaz switched over to the other line. When she switched back over to Damion, there was a Double-A representative on the line.

"Hello, Double-A, how can I help you?"

Damion smiled. His mother was always on point. Why hadn't he thought of the three-way call himself? Three-way calling was used more often than not when a nigga was locked up. Devon came up with a believable story in a matter of minutes.

Jaz held the phone to her ear in shock. She never knew how good of a liar her son was. *Damn, he's good,* she thought, as she continued to listen in on his conversation.

The representative had taken all the information regarding Damion's stolen vehicle. You could hear her busy at work on her computer.

"Please hold on a second," the rep spoke into her headpiece. She pushed a few buttons, stroked a few more keys, and there on the screen was the exact location of Damion's Lexus SUV. "Mr. Aviles, I found your truck. It is somewhere in the middle of nowhere. Someplace like a field."

"How do you know that?"

"'Cause there are no known addresses in that area."

"Okay, then what county?"

"Your vehicle in somewhere upstate in a town called Ossining."

"Ossining?"

"Yes, sir, Ossining, New York."

"You got to be kidding."

"No, sir, I am not kidding. Would you like for me to inform the authorities out in that area?"

"No," Damion yelled into the receiver, now standing up. Damion did not need for Devon to be picked up for grand theft auto. "I'll take care of this myself. Thank you so much for your help."

"You're welcome, sir. We are always here to handle all of your needs."

"Be careful what you ask for, young lady, you just might get it."

Embarrassed by Damion's last statement, the rep quickly disconnected her call. Damion couldn't help but laugh.

Jaz mimicked the rep's line. "We are always here to handle all of your needs."

"Mom, please, we ain't got time for any of your weird shit."

"Okay, okay. Now what?"

"Get everybody together and go out there and search the fields, farms, any and all deserted areas. He has to be out there somewhere."

"Dey, do you think he went after Supreme and those other guys?"

"Yes, I do. Devon is not one to give up so easy. You know that, Mom. So, get your ass out there."

"Watch your mouth. I'm still your mother."

Jaz's smile could have reached the stars. She loved her son more than he realized.

"Mom, please."

"Okay, baby, I am on my way."

Jaz hung up, and then dialed the code into her celly. In less than thirty minutes, all of the Geechies would be at her front door, ready for action. She also called Mark. She needed him again. Toni was nowhere to be found. Jaz wasn't going to take time out to figure it out either. Stroking Toni's ego was not on the agenda. Jaz explained her current reality to Mark, and he agreed to meet her. Mark would have waited a lifetime for the chance to help his son again.

* * * * *

Supreme's pulse was weak. If he didn't get medical treatment soon, it was a great possibility that he wouldn't make it. He could die of internal injuries. Devon sensed that Supreme was not going to make it. So, he swung into action. He took the tape recorder out of his pocket and walked over

217

to where Supreme lay out on the floor. Slapping him softly on the face, Devon searched for a response.

"Yo, one of you little niggas get me some water or something. This nigga is out cold."

Scoop ran over to a well, dipped the bucket into its tunnel, and drew water. He ran back and threw it at Supreme's face, causing him to gag, coughing uncontrollably. Supreme had come back to life.

"Wake up, nigga!" Devon yelled at him. "Get your ass up. We are far from finished."

Supreme opened his eyes, looked at Devon, then tried to speak, but his words were a mere whisper. It was painful.

"What, nigga? I don't hear you," Devon said, leaning in closer and placing his ear to Supreme's mouth.

Again, Supreme tried to talk. Devon leaned in a little bit closer. Supreme's words might have been nothing but a whisper, but his message got across loud and clear. He asked Devon not to kill him.

"Why shouldn't I, Sup? You didn't have a problem trying to take me out. All I want from you is to talk into this little recorder. Tell me how you put a hit out on me and how your people almost killed my brother. Tell me how badly you wanted me out of the way so that you could take control of Spanish Harlem."

Devon's mouth was fuming. He was beyond pissed the fuck off.

"If I do all of this that you are asking, will you let me go, Dee?" Supreme fought to catch his breath.

If Devon didn't know better, he could have sworn that Supreme's ribs were broken, making it hard for him to breathe. Devon grilled him. He wanted nothing more than to end this nigga's pathetic life.

"Yeah, man, I'll let you go." Devon pressed the recorder. "Talk, Supreme, before I put these young eager niggas on your ass again."

With all of the strength that Supreme could muster, he began talking into the tape recorder.

When he finally finished confessing, Devon looked at him squarely and said, "I always knew you were a bitch-ass nigga."

Devon stood up and walked away with the tape tightly tucked into his jeans pocket. Giving Toy and his people the eye, Devon walked out of the old abandoned barn without a second glance.

Sexy

Chapter 32

Venus crawled out of the warm tub Brenda had prepared for her. She wrapped herself in one of the many towels Brenda had neatly folded on the bathroom shelves. Brenda had made it a point from day one to make Venus feel at home. And after everything that had gone down today, that's exactly how she felt.

It felt good to know that she belonged somewhere. Damion sure as hell had made her feel completely out of place. Venus could not for the life of her get the scene out of her mind. Over the course of the day, she could only envision the difference in Damion's behavior. It didn't sit right with her. It was as though she was dealing with a complete stranger, a different person altogether. Venus sat on the edge of the tub holding her head between her hands, eyes swollen from crying.

"Something just isn't right!" she said over and over again.

"What do you mean something ain't right?" Brenda stated as she entered the bathroom. "Listen, girl, it is better that you got to see that no-good-nigga's true colors before you got all caught up in him."

"I'm already all caught up in him, Bee."

"Oh, no, you ain't. You just think you are. There is a whole world out there full of fine-ass brothas you have yet to meet."

"No, Brenda, you don't understand. There is something really weird going on."

"Like what?"

"I don't know."

"That's because ain't shit going on. That nigga was no good." Brenda bent down in front of Venus, who was becoming more like a little sister than a very special friend. "Venus, lift your head a minute. Look at yourself. You are ready to make yourself sick over a man you don't even know."

Venus lifted her head and looked at Brenda with tears in her eyes. She didn't have any of the answers to all of her questions. All she knew was that there was more to the story. She had spent enough time with Damion to know that he was far from thuggish. He was nothing but a gentleman at all times. The man that she was with today was not the man she had spent countless hours with. The tenderness he shared with her after she told him about her past was not the beast she had met today.

"Brenda, what if I tell you that I honestly don't believe that Damion was Damion."

"What!" Brenda looked at Venus like she had thirty heads.

"What if I tell you that I don't think it was Damion who did all that crazy shit today?"

"Then who the fuck was it? His brother is locked up, right?"

"Yeah, supposed to be, anyway."

"Girl, what the fuck are you thinking?"

After leaving the bathroom, Brenda and Venus proceeded to the kitchen, where Brenda grabbed the bottle of Chardonnay sitting on the counter. She took two of her tallest glasses and began to fill them to the rim. Venus sat down at the dining room table waiting for Brenda to join her.

"I don't know. I just have the strangest feeling about all of this." Venus grabbed the glass from Brenda's extended hand and took a long swig of the white wine. "Damn that shit burns!" Venus said, placing her hands on her throat. Her throat felt like it was on fire. "I should have figured that shit out the day he had come to see me. You remember, right? The day I wore the red cat suit?"

"Yeah, I remember." Brenda sat opposite her now, listening not only with her ears but with her body.

"Well, when he pulled up, he acted as though I was the forbidden fruit. I tried everything to get him to stay or take me along with him. He outright refused to have anything to do with me that day."

"Maybe he had other plans."

"Nah, he was different. He even looked different, now that I think about it."

"But aren't they identical twins?"

"My understanding is that no one can tell them apart. That's why Devon is locked up for murder."

"I don't understand. I wish you would stop talking in riddles."

"Okay, listen. About four years ago, some guy named Supreme put a hit out on Devon."

"Supreme?"

"Yeah, listen. Anyway, at their Aunt Trouble's wedding, the hit man mistook Damion for Devon and shot at him. Devon then turned around and shot at the hit man, killing him instantly."

"Girl, this shit sounds crazy." Brenda was leaning in closer, holding on to Venus's every word.

"Yeah, I know. Anyway, all this crazy-ass shit started a few days ago, and it's getting crazier by the minute."

"So what do you think is going on?" Brenda asked, while filling their glasses again.

"What if they found a way to switch places?"

"How? Devon is locked up in a max, girl. You are losing your fuckin' mind now, for real. Venus, there is no way that they could do something like that."

"I don't know. Anything is possible. All I know is that was not Damion today."

Brenda pushed her chair back, walked over to the phone, lifted it, and handed it over to Venus.

"There is only one way to find out."

"How?" Venus asked.

"Call their mother."

"I can't do that."

"Why not? Don't you want to know what the fuck is going on?"

"Yeah."

"Well, then, call."

Venus took the phone, stared at the numbers, and then lowered her head in confusion.

"Don't just sit there. Call. Because if you don't, I will."

* * * * *

While Jaz waited for the Geechies to show up, she sat looking through some old photo albums. Damion and Devon at age one. Then again at age two. Who would have thought her sons would have found themselves caught up in so much chaos? She never wanted them to lose their innocence. This is one of the reasons Jaz had changed her life around. Jaz never wanted her sons to experience the pain of ever having to see the inside of a prison. When Devon chose to live the life of a drug dealer, she felt like her heart had been torn apart.

Toni and Jaz sat so many nights praying that their son would be safe out on the streets. She cried; she prayed; she even fought him on occasion, but nothing worked. So when she felt that she had lost the battle, Jaz silently vowed to ride and die for him, if ever need be.

Jaz had put the word out to all of the old-timers in the neighborhood, asking them to protect her son on the down-low. Devon was never put up on the fact that he had a few angels looking out for him. Jaz knew where her son was at all times. The guilt of not knowing that her son's life had a price tag devastated her. How could something as serious as this have passed her by? Her tears now fell into the pages and onto the faces of the sons she loved so much.

Jaz was jerked back into reality by the sound of her ringing phone. She didn't have the energy to walk over and pick it up, but she had to. She placed the photo album down after she kissed their little faces.

"Hello!"

"Hello, Ms. Jaz?"

"Yes, who's this?"

"This is Venus. Can I please talk to you for a minute?"

"I don't think this is a good time, Venus."

"Please, I need a few minutes of your time." Venus did not want to be rejected again, so she continued. "I need to talk to you about what happened today, about Damion."

"What about him?"

"Ms. Jaz, that wasn't Damion today, was it?"

Venus held her breath as she heard Jaz sigh.

"I don't know what you're talking about."

"I think you do. I'm not stupid. That was not the man I fell in love with. Before you say anything, please just listen to what I have to say."

Jaz listened to Venus go on and on about the difference in her sons. Venus had nailed it right on the head. However, she was not about to let her know that she was right. Saved by the bell, Jaz politely told Venus that she was barking up the wrong tree. She told her that she had a great imagination and should use her talents of storytelling to write books. Jaz hated to be rude to Venus, but she had to go. She could hear in her voice how much she really loved Damion, but she would leave all that explaining up to her son. Jaz was not about to cross that line. And, besides, she didn't have time to baby-sit. She had to go find Devon.

The Geechies entered the apartment along with Mark closely behind them. After much debate on what to do and how to do it, they headed up north in search of Devon. With all the information given to her by the Double-A representative, they cruised along the Deegan Expressway.

About forty-five minutes into the ride, Jaz noticed Damion's truck pass them by on the opposite side of the road. She had to take a second look to make sure. Sure enough the license plate number belonged to Damion. It read, "Playa4Life." It was one of the many gifts Devon had showered him with. It was not a coincidence, the truck, the plate. Nah, it was definitely Devon heading back into the city.

"Stop the truck, Mark?"

"What?"

"Stop the fuckin' truck and turn this motherfucker around. Devon is heading back to the city!"

"What the fuck are you talking about?"

The Geechies were now all looking behind them, trying to see what Jaz thought she saw.

"There, look, that's Damion's truck. Turn this motherfucker around, Mark, now," Jaz screamed into his face.

"All right, chill, I got you."

Mark turned into a rest stop, then began to drive the truck in reverse, causing the truck to move backwards. It would be easier if he headed back to the last exit they had passed since the next exit was about a mile ahead. Quickly, he made it off the ramp, turning on to the southbound side while Jaz searched for her cell phone, but couldn't find it. She had forgotten to grab her phone.

"Somebody pass me their phone."

226

Instantly, she had six phones staring her in the face.

"Thank you, guys. I knew I could count on you."

Jaz smiled as she grabbed one.

* * * * *

Devon reached for the ringing celly.

"Yeah," he answered without looking at the caller ID. All he was worried about was getting the hell back into the city. Familiar ground was what he craved.

"Dee, where are you?"

"Ma, I am on my way to see you."

"No, baby, where are you?"

"I'm on the Deegan. Why?"

"Look behind you, baby."

"What?"

"Look behind you. As a matter of fact, look to your left."

"Oh, shit. What the fuck are you guys doing out here?"

Devon couldn't believe what he was looking at. It was his mother, his father, and the Geechies all cramped up in her SUV.

"Looking for you. Pull over, Devon!"

"Nah, man, we need to get back. You are not going to believe what I'm about to tell you."

"What?"

"I got the confession from Supreme."

"You got to be kidding. How? When? Where? Never mind. Oh, shit, guys, Devon got Supreme to talk!" Jaz was hollering back at the Geechies. "Baby, you are up for a new hearing soon. The judge granted your appeal!"

"Get the fuck out of here!"

"Yeah, Damion called me today with the good news."

"Ma, do you know what this means?"

"Yes, baby. It means you are coming home."

"Yeah, Ma, I am coming home."

Sexy

Devon couldn't believe the words that had escaped his mother's lips. God was good. Life was going to be even better.

Chapter 33

At the courthouse, Devon, Jaz, and Mark sat outside waiting for the doors to open. At exactly nine a.m., each courtroom would be open and ready for business. Devon was ready, too. He had never been more ready for anything in his life like he was at this very moment.

Dressed in a gray Armani suit complete with shoes and tie, he was able to fit right in. He looked just like one of the many attorneys who stood nearby, drinking coffee with one hand and holding a briefcase in the other. Some read newspapers, briefs, or other legal documents, while others negotiated with one another, trying to come to some kind of agreement, a plea bargain. In their briefcases they possessed the outcome of any one given individual, the client. In Devon's possession was the key to gain his freedom. It was not guaranteed to work, but with the new evidence, the judge was sure to see that all of this was done in self-defense.

The evidence would have to be brought forward with care, though. One mistake on his part and Damion would be discovered, something neither one of them could afford. The evening that he gained the information from Supreme, he went straight to his mom's crib in hopes that his brother would call back. He did, they talked, and finally, phase two of Devon's plan was put into motion. They would continue to play their parts out until the very end. Devon could hear the clicking of the locks as the court C.O.'s opened the front doors to 100 Centre Street. Jaz rested her hand on Devon's thigh, letting him know in so many words that it was show time.

"Are you ready?"

"As ready as I'll ever be."

Together they stood up, and then headed for the line that started forming. Mark fell back, admiring his son and mother. He had to admit that he felt a little out of place. He wanted to be angry at Jaz for refusing him his right as a father. The anger that he felt for so many years had now turned into something he couldn't put into words. All he knew was that at this particular moment he only felt admiration for her. She had proved to be one hell of a mother, and his sons were very lucky to have her.

"Come on, Mark!" Jaz looked back at him. "Don't just sit there. I know you don't think we are going to stand on this long-ass line. Use your badge to get us through."

Jaz's smile went right through him. *She still has spunk,* Mark thought to himself, as he reached into his coat pocket.

"The Honorable Judge Ramirez is now presiding. Everyone please stand," the bailiff yelled throughout the courtroom.

Once the judge was seated on his throne, the bailiff instructed us to take our seats, as well. It was a matter of respect for the higher authority. But how could anyone respect a system that never respected the men and women who stood before them?

As Devon looked around the courtroom, he noticed that there were only two families sitting out in the audience, his people and a family of four who looked to him as though they would fall apart at any moment. Winning an appeal was rare in New York State, but not impossible. He said a silent prayer for them.

The first case on the calendar was his, Devon Aviles vs. the New York State Supreme Court. When he heard his name, he immediately turned his head. His eyes connected with Damion, who was being escorted into the courtroom. The die-for-you bond between them was transparent.

To Devon's surprise, Damion looked good. He had underestimated Damion completely. He thought that Damion doing time would affect him in some sort of way. His physique was overbearing and strong. Dressed in a pair of beige khakis, white linen shirt, and white uptowns, he walked as though he were the one wearing the five-thousand dollar suit. His head was held high, unafraid of what the outcome might be. It was all in God's hands now.

"Order in the court," the judge said, as he began their judicial session. The moment had arrived.

"Good morning, ladies and gentlemen. Today, we are here to review Devon Aviles' request to vacate his sentence of twenty-five years to life. Mr. Padilla, can you please approach the bench?"

Mr. Padilla tapped Damion's arm and told him to sit tight, while he walked over to the stand before the magistrate judge.

"Mr. Padilla, I have here in front of me the brief that you drafted concerning your client. You are aware that the grounds on this appeal are likely not to be considered."

"Yes, Your Honor, I understand this. However, if you will allow me to show the burden of proof, I'm sure you will see that my client was acting in self-defense."

"Mr. Padilla, I assure you that I am fully aware of the case. You may proceed. Good luck."

Mr. Padilla walked back over to Damion, who seemed to look blank now. Pale was more like it. All of the color had drained from his face. A slight smile appeared, though, when Mr. Padilla winked in his direction.

The attorney then proceeded to open his briefcase. In hand, he held several documents, which he handed over to the prosecutor. The prosecutor, a Ms. Kim something-or-other, had a reputation of deliberately misleading grand juries and witnesses for her own personal gain. She was known to stack bogus charges on an indictment in order to mislead the defendant and induce a guilty plea.

That had not been the case for Devon. Devon had been found guilty by a group of his peers, twelve civilians who knew nothing of the law. On pure hearsay, he was convicted to twenty-five years of imprisonment. Not once did they acknowledge his intent. Now, his attorney had a second chance to introduce factual instruments instead of the false ones Ms. Kim had introduced during Devon's first trial. Under oath, all witnesses would testify once again on what really happened that night at Club Ecstasy. Mr. Padilla would address all past testimonies and bring forth new ones.

Devon looked on with piercing eyes. His mind drifted back to that very first court scene. He remembered how his attorney's words had echoed throughout. *Your Honor, with all due respect, the defendant's actions cannot legitimately be addressed by hearsay and affidavit. Hearsay is not evidence. Trial by affidavit cannot be condoned where bona fide issues of fact are being presented.* These challenging words represented nothing at the time. Devon's fate was handed to him through sheer ignorance. Yet, still in the hands of the Supreme Court, Devon's fate would be once again put to the test.

Devon felt a little discomfort. He tried to place his mind back on the here and now. So far, nothing was said of the tape he held securely between his hands. In an instant, Mr. Padilla began to call upon errors permitted by A.D.A. Kim. The court appeared to have introduced new principles in an all-new criminal procedure. The judge listened without interruptions, lowering his glasses from time to time to look at Damion, who was now looking back at Devon. Damion didn't need to say a word. Devon could feel his distress.

Together, they searched for a little reassurance. Suddenly, they heard the judge call out Damion's name.

"Yes, sir," Devon said, jumping to his feet.

"You can now come forward with this new evidence."

Devon's hands began to sweat. Deep down, he needed to play this smoothly. Cautioned by his mother's touch, he walked up to the altar of the courtroom and handed the tape over to the attorney. Devon and Damion both watched as he inserted it into the tape player. The room fell silent waiting to hear what would come through the loudspeaker.

Venus had snuck in during the court's proceeding. No one seemed to notice that she sat quietly in the last row of seats. They were all in deep concentration, listening to Supreme's voice ring throughout the room. Pleas for help could be heard as he described his plan to kill Devon. Not one person read in between the lines, but Venus knew that at that moment Supreme was begging for his life. Thoughts of how Damion must have gotten him to talk made her body stiffen with fear.

While sitting in the courtroom, visions of her court trial came to mind. This was the last place she wanted to be, but she had to know. She wanted to know the truth. Venus wanted to confirm her suspicions.

Everyone looked pretty normal for the most part. Could these brothers look so much alike that no one could tell the difference, including her? That was a scary thought. How could she not know which one was which? Which one was the one she wanted to spend the rest of her life with? Her eyes moved from one figure to the other.

Jaz and Mark didn't show their emotions, either. Jaz just sat there in awe. Mark's eyes were looking straight ahead, revealing nothing. Venus wanted so badly to move up the aisle to join them. Leaning forward, she listened patiently and waited patiently to hear a "not guilty" verdict. Gradually, the tape had come to an end, and Devon walked back to his seat to wait.

"This court will be in recess for one hour, in which time everyone will return for my decision."

Venus stood up and exited the courtroom. She had decided to stay incognito until the time was right.

Chapter 34

Unaware of his destiny, Damion continued to sit quietly in the bull-pens (holding cells) that lay low between the concrete walls of the criminal courthouse. Looking at his surroundings, he noticed that the walls were filled with graffiti. There were names and years of convicts who had traveled down the same road. As he waited for the C.O. to announce when court would be back in process, Damion had time to be alone to think.

What if something went wrong? What if the judge felt that Supreme's confession was not enough to let him go? What would Devon do then? How would they switch back? That was the main question on Damion's mind. What if they couldn't switch back? Was he willing to live his life impersonating his brother? Was he willing to give up everything he worked so hard for? What was the ultimate sacrifice? Was he willing to give up his name, his manhood forever? What choice did he have if Devon lost this trial?

Damion quickly stood before the gates as he heard his brother's name being called out.

"The court will now come to order," the bailiff said again.

Damion was being escorted out of the holding cells. When he entered the courtroom, this time he sensed that something wasn't right. He searched for a clue in the faces of the people that represented the system. But, there was nothing. No sign of emotions, just the blank images of the courtroom personnel scattering back and forth. Mr. Michael Padilla stood before the defense table holding a white handkerchief, which he used on occasion to wipe away the moisture that built up on his forehead from time to time. Everyone who mattered waited with anticipation for the judge to announce his decision.

Damion saw Devon and their mother sitting behind the attorney. *Where is the man who was sitting with them earlier? Who is he anyway?* Damion tried to figure out as he continued to move forward.

Mark had chosen to sit outside of the courtroom with the Geechies, who had arrived at the courthouse in time for the verdict. They would not have missed this day for anything in the world. Jaz was going to need their support if they didn't release Damion/Devon.

Jaz sat still with her head held high, as she watched her son walk into the courtroom with pride. Her son had class. It didn't matter where they placed him. His style shined through. Her son would never let you see him sweat. He could handle just about anything that was thrown his way. Jaz couldn't help but be proud of him. It took a real man to do what he was doing.

Devon, on the other hand, was nervous, and for the first time since this all began, afraid, really afraid. He was afraid that all of his efforts would be for nothing. He glanced into his brother's eyes right before he took his place at the table. With them no words needed to be spoken. Damion knew. The creases that formed between Devon's eyebrows were deep. He looked as though he had aged some in the past hour. Lack of sleep had a lot to do with it, too.

Several hours before the court appearance, Toy had called Devon to tell him that his boys Brooklyn, Jack, and Scoop had been arrested on some old robbery charges.

Devon wasn't really concerned about them. The fellas had been paid to help him get the information. What they did with Supreme was no concern of his, either. If anything, he was fully aware that they could pretty much handle their business. What concerned him was having any of them linked back to him. Not a great possibility. How he had obtained the confession from Supreme had not been questioned yet, although he wasn't certain if someone from the D.A.'s office would bring up the credibility of the evidence. The thought did come to mind, though.

"Everyone, please rise. The Honorable Judge Ramirez is now presiding."

"You may all take your seats," Judge Ramirez instructed the family, "except you, Mr. Aviles. I don't see any reason to prolong this trial any further. What's been brought forth as newly discovered evidence has been accepted by the court."

Jaz's eyes opened wide as she held her breath and reached out for Devon, who looked like he was about to jump out of his seat. Damion turned his head to look at his mother. It was a big possibility that in a few seconds he could have his life back.

The judge continued. "The post trial motions your attorney has entered on your behalf seek various forms of relief, but they generally requested a new trial, which you are having right now. Because the charge that you were indicted for is serious, I have taken it upon myself to use my own discretion as well as many years of experience to guide me in making this decision."

Everyone in the courtroom fell silent as the judge shuffled through some paper. He adjusted his glasses, and then continued.

"I am dropping the charge of murder in the first to manslaughter in the second degree. Mr. Aviles, I am going to sentence you under the new guidelines of the penal law. Do you have any objections, Mr. Padilla?" The judge looked from one to the other.

"No, sir," they both said, as they smiled at each other.

"Mr. Aviles, I am sentencing you to four years in a New York State correctional facility for manslaughter in the second degree, running concurrent with one year determined sentence on your criminal possession of a weapon. Do you understand your new sentence, Mr. Aviles?"

The numbers sounded good to him, but he didn't have a fucking clue as to what was happening.

"Young man, do you understand or not?"

Damion looked straight at the judge's face and said, "No, Your Honor."

"It means, Mr. Aviles, as of yesterday, you have been incarcerated at Sing-Sing for four years. Is that correct?"

"Yes, Your Honor."

"Well, then what that means is that you have completed your time. Mr. Aviles, you are free to go."

Before Damion was able to turn around and walk out, all shit had broken loose. Venus had been sitting in the courtroom the whole time, but Damion had been too busy to notice her. He kept looking at his mother, who sat there with tears flowing from her eyes.

Venus kind of envied their relationship. She had always wanted her mother to look at her in the same way. Unfortunately, drugs and the streets had taken her mind way too fast. She never got the chance to see it coming her way.

Venus listened closely to what the judge was saying. Once she heard that he was free to go, she jumped up from her seat. She adjusted her coat, walked straight up to the front where Jaz and Devon stood to meet Damion, and stood there. When Damion turned around he looked dumbfounded, but once their eyes met, tears of joy flowed. Venus had been so angered and hurt over all of the bullshit that she didn't know what to do. Slap the shit out of him or curse his ass out? Venus had been contemplating all kinds of shit. Now, as she stood frozen, mesmerized by Damion's coffee-colored eyes, all she could do was cry.

Epilogue

Six Months Later:

• Jaz and Toni talked things out and are back together again. They are the happiest they have been in a long time.

• Mark got to meet his other son, Damion, and became a part of their lives.

• Devon is still single and doing him. After four years of being down, he just wants to lay low and take it easy. He has invested some money with Dirty Music Entertainment and is still looking into other businesses to venture out in. The legal way!

• As for Damion and Venus…well, she had given him a run for his money. However, once Damion explained, she had to give in. In the end, she couldn't resist his charm. Plans of a wedding are in the air.

• Marcus got a surprise visit from his two favorite people, Damion and Devon. Along with them, they brought Venus, who had known for a fact, once she heard Damion out, that Marcus was her brother. You had to be on that V.I. to believe it.

• Jack, Brooklyn, and Scoop were incarcerated at the Albany County Jail. This is where they were discovered. They were not niggas at all. They were dykes dressed in men's clothing. They were lesbian women on the prowl.

• The Geechies continued on in their everyday routine of being fly and getting paid. Club Ecstasy is one of the hottest clubs in NYC. They have some of the biggest playas coming in the place, so if you ever feel mischievous and want to party, stop on by. They will be waiting on your arrival.

ORDER FORM

Mail to: Déjà vu Publications
P.O. Box 1002
New York, N.Y. 10029

Name _____

Street Address _____

City/State/Zip _____

TITLE	PRICE	QUANTITY
A Better Touch by Sexy	$14.95	
Twofold by Sexy	$14.95	
Uptown Menace to Hell and Back by Carmen Noboa-Espinal	$14.95	

SHIPPING/HANDLING: ADD $4.60 per book
(Shipped via U.S. Media Mail)
TOTAL: $_____

FORMS OF ACCEPTED PAYMENTS:
Institutional checks & money orders are preferred methods of payment. Déjà Vu Publications does NOT recommend sending cash through the postal system.

Contact Publisher directly about discounting availability for special bulk orders (ten book minimum).

Déjà Vu Publications is now accepting manuscripts.
Contact Deborah Cardona at the address above for more information on how to submit your novels.

Sexy

TWOFOLD

Sexy